Fifth Wheel

Samantha Baca

Just One Time

Second Chances

Third Time's The Charm

Four-ever Single

Fifth Wheel

Cover Design: Richard Baca
Image(s): DepositPhotos

Contents

Contents

<u>One</u>
Lia

"So, what are your plans for the day?" Bella asked as I held the phone between my ear and shoulder as I rummaged through the fridge. I closed it, frowning at the lack of food in it.

"I'm going to take a shower and then start looking for an apartment," I answered, still feeling weird rummaging through the cabinets when this wasn't *technically* my house.

I had been staying with my best friend at her new husband's house for about a month now after my house unexpectedly caught fire. While the initial report had been that a damaged extension cord caused it, they later found that the house had several things that weren't up to code, and it was deemed unlivable for the next few months until repairs were made.

"Lia, you don't have to rush to move out. Jones already told you that you can stay with us as long as you need."

"Yeah, but I don't want to take advantage of that. It's been nice of him to let me crash here, but we all know it's not a forever thing. I have some time before I start my new job, so why not use that time to do something productive?"

"Because you've been busting your butt in med school and finally have a break from your clinical rotations for the summer. You should do something fun. Live life, take some downtime. You have two weeks off before you start a new job with the house to yourself while we're gone; don't waste it."

While I was excited to have some time to myself, I knew that it was only short-lived while Bella and Jones were on their honeymoon. They were supposed to go to a lake house in New Hampshire right after the wedding, but the house ended up flooding, and they got stuck in Beaumont Creek. The guys at the firehouse pulled together and surprised Jones and Bella with an all-inclusive trip this summer, making it the first honeymoon before they went to Italy this winter on their second.

"By myself?" I asked, cradling the phone in my neck. "You're off living the life on some tropical beach, probably still having mind-blowing sex with your husband while Kensy is going on wine-tasting excursions with my stupid brother in California. I'm just stuck here in boring ol' Beaumont Creek with no one to hang out with."

"I'm sorry, Lia. I told you to come with us."

"On your *honeymoon?* No thanks. It's bad enough being the fifth wheel when you guys are all in town. I'm not about to be the pathetic loser who crashes her best friend's honeymoon."

"You're not pathetic, and you're not a fifth wheel. But you do have time to yourself, so embrace it. Do something relaxing for once. Go get a massage. Hang out at the beach. There are lots of things you can do. You have a break, so take it."

"You and I both know that while it sounds good, it's not realistic," I replied, opening the cabinet by the kitchen window to grab a coffee mug. My hand froze in the air as I stared outside, my eyes nearly bulging out of my head as I stared at the man in the driveway. "I gotta go."

I didn't wait for Bella to acknowledge me before I hung up and shoved my phone into my pocket before storming out the front door.

"What the hell do you think you're doing here?" I demanded, hands firmly on my hips as I glared at him and his stupid, perfect face as he grinned at me. "What? You don't harass me enough at work, so now you have to stalk me at home?"

He leaned back on the hood of his car and crossed his ankles casually as he held a stack of mail in his hands.

I raised my eyebrows, getting increasingly frustrated by his lack of response.

"Hellloooo. Don't you think you owe me an answer?"

He rubbed his lips together and then pushed off the car and invaded my space.

"You don't live there." He pointed behind me. Out of everything I just said, *that* was what he was choosing to focus on?

"As a matter of fact, I do. And you seem to know that, or you wouldn't be here *stalking* me. So, what is it, Doc? Do you have some strange obsession with me and just can't help yourself, so you're going to follow me all over town now that I'm off for summer break?"

"Hate to break it to you, Lia, but the only person doing any stalking around here is *you*."

"What?!" I asked as an incredulous laugh slipped out.

He nodded his head, stepping even closer.

"Unlike you, I actually live here. In that house," he said as he pointed to the one next door. The one whose driveway his stupid car was parked in. "I've lived there for years, whereas you've only been *living* in this one for about a month."

"You sure know a lot for not stalking anyone," I muttered, lifting my hand to shield my eyes from the sun.

"Yeah, well, maybe *I'm* not the real stalker," he teased, his blue eyes glimmering in the sunlight.

"Oh, please. Don't flatter yourself. You couldn't pay me to stalk you." *Though the money wouldn't hurt.*

He shrugged and then tilted his head to the side, his eyes looking at me mockingly before he spoke. I tried to ignore the fact that I noticed he got a haircut this morning, especially when my fingers itched to reach out and touch the soft fade.

"Are you trying to say that it's purely a coincidence that you suddenly moved into the house right next door to me as the semester comes to an end? Call me crazy, but I think that you just couldn't stand the thought of not seeing me for a few months at the hospital, so you devised a plan to make sure you were still in close proximity so *you* could easily stalk *me*."

My nostrils flared as I stepped back, my irritation growing even thicker.

"You're so arrogant."

"Yet you can't seem to stay away." He smirked, knowing he was getting under my skin.

"Whatever." I shook my head and turned to leave. "See you later, *Dr. Dickhead*."

It was bold to call him that, but given that we weren't at the hospital and I wasn't currently in my clinical rotation, it didn't matter.

"It's Mason," he called out as I walked off.

I stopped and looked at him over my shoulder.

"My name is Mason." He stood there staring at me with those deep blue eyes lighting up with his dimpled grin.

"Are you saying you don't like the nickname I picked for you?"

I didn't wait for him to answer before I stormed off and slammed the door shut behind me.

<u>Two</u>
Lia

I pushed my shopping cart aggressively through the aisles, frustrated that I was home by myself for the next two weeks and had no one that I could drag to Tipsy Taquito because my best friends had abandoned me. I tried to convince myself that this was a time for self-growth and that I would focus on eating healthy and working out while I had the time, but that already proved to be a lie as I grabbed a bottle of premade margaritas and added it to the cart filled with junk food.

My morning had been wasted trying to find someplace to live with there being a housing shortage in Beaumont Creek. The only places available were either in a bad part of town, or the rent was so high I would have to sell organs on the black market just to afford the deposit and first month's payment.

I knew that I couldn't stay with Jones and Bella forever, but I also didn't want to give in and move in with my parents again. They were finally empty nesters and were starting to enjoy their time alone together, so I didn't want to ruin that. It was like no matter where I went, I was always the odd one out. The fifth wheel that just never belonged and everyone felt sorry for.

I rounded the corner and scanned the packaged frozen meat, debating on what I felt like cooking this week. I reached for a package of ground beef and then put it back when I knew I would just end up depressed when my tacos weren't as good as the ones at Tipsy Taquito. I grabbed a few packs of chicken breasts and then made my way to the produce section.

By the time I got home, it was already lunchtime, and I was starving. I didn't want to bother with cooking anything, so I grabbed a bowl and fixed milk and cereal, deciding it was healthier than getting fast food. If I was going to focus on taking care of myself then I needed to stop making excuses and taking the easy way out.

After I was done, I loaded the dishwasher and started it, feeling good about being so domesticated. I had considered going to the gym and working out, but then I remembered that Jones still had a treadmill in the other spare bedroom.

I ran for an hour before jumping in the shower to clean up. My phone was playing a mix of old hip-hop and R&B music, which had me dancing along as the hot water ran down my skin. I reached for the bottle of shampoo and held it in front of me like a microphone as I belted out a mind-blowing rendition of a Mariah Carey chart-topper. It didn't bother me that the bathroom window was open because the fresh air was nice, and it kept it from getting too steamy in the bathroom—which I hated.

My fingers gripped the bottle as I squirted some shampoo into my hand, slathering it on my head as I leaned to the side to put the bottle back on the shelf. I closed my eyes as I massaged my scalp with my nails, still dancing to the music when I bumped the bottle and knocked it to the floor. Not wanting to get shampoo in my eyes, I left the bottle for a few seconds while I finished rinsing my hair, not knowing that it had opened and was leaking all over the shower floor.

I turned to rinse my face and immediately felt my feet slip out from under me as I went flying forward, gripping along the wall of the tiled walk-in shower to stop myself, but couldn't. My left ankle bent at an awkward angle before the pain began radiating through my leg as a loud scream erupted from my lungs.

I managed to turn the water off as I clung to the side of the shower, holding onto one of the built-in shelves while keeping my leg from touching anything. The music was still playing, but I couldn't reach my phone from where I was without putting weight on my foot.

"Shit," I muttered, trying to take a deep, calming breath even though I felt anything but calm. "Alexis, turn off the music."

I waited for a few seconds, but it kept going.

"Alex, turn off the music," I tried instead, not remembering the name of the voice-activated command thing on my phone. "Alice, turn off the music."

I tossed my head back and focused on my breathing as chills ran over my body, partly from the lack of warmth the water was providing and mostly from the pain I was in. I knew it would only be a few minutes before I would have to give in and sit down because my body wouldn't be able to hold my weight on one leg any longer. It was too risky to try to hobble out of the shower, knowing the chances I would fall again would be even greater. At this rate, I was going to die in the guest bathroom, stuck naked in the shower for the local firefighters to find when someone called in and reported a foul odor.

"Alexander," I shouted, my strength quickly fading. "Fucking whoever you are—turn off the music!"

"What's wrong?" a male voice asked as the music immediately stopped.

"Alexander, I need you to call 911," I replied with a shaky breath as I stared at the floor, oblivious to the person in the bathroom with me.

"What happened?"

My head whipped up at the sudden realization, knocking me off balance again as I struggled to hold my foot up.

"MASON! Go away!" I shrieked, trying to cover myself as the shower door slid open.

"Lia, you obviously need help. Now, I don't know who Alexander is, but I can tell by the swelling around your ankle that you somehow broke it. Grab onto my neck so I can help you out."

"Not in a million years," I sobbed, turning my head so he wouldn't see me cry.

"Stop being difficult, and let me help you."

"No. Just hand me my phone, and I'll call for help."

He folded his arms over his chest as he stared at me with an arched eyebrow.

"Who are you going to call?"

"911."

"And then what do you think will happen?"

"They'll put me in the ambulance and take me to the hospital," I snapped, already hating where this was going.

"And who do you think is going to help you when you get there?"

"An ER doctor," I gritted through my teeth.

"You mean like the one standing in front of you?"

I sighed heavily, feeling my body grow heavier as I fought back the tears stinging my eyes again.

"Stop being so damn difficult, Lia," Mason growled before stepping into the shower and gently picking me up, making sure not to touch my injured ankle.

Embarrassment rushed through me as my wet, naked body was pressed against his as he gently set me on the counter and grabbed the towel from the hook behind him. He didn't even glance at my body as he shoved it at me, his focus immediately going to my ankle as he bent down in front of me.

"I'm pretty sure it's broken, but we'll need to get you to the hospital for x-rays to confirm."

"Okay," I said, tucking the towel around my body awkwardly to cover myself the best I could. "Thanks for your help. I'll call for an ambulance, and you can go on your way."

"I'll drive you."

"You don't need to do that. I'm fine calling and waiting for a ride."

"I will drive you," he insisted, standing in front of me with his expression stern like I'd seen plenty of times while on rotation in the ER.

"I don't want to make you go out of your way. It's fine really. If you can just help me to the front door, I'll wait for them to come."

"Lia, I'm on call tonight, which means the minute you get there, they're going to call me to come in anyway. So why not just cut the bullshit, and I'll drive you there myself."

I pulled the towel tighter against my body, hating that I was in this situation to begin with.

It was embarrassing to let Dr. Dickhead dress me, but once we got to the hospital and they gave me a strong pain medication, I didn't care about anything in the world.

<u>Three</u>
Mason

It took a few hours at the hospital for them to set Lia's ankle in a cast and go over what she could and could not do until it came off in four to eight weeks. Thankfully, the fracture wasn't bad enough that she needed surgery, but she would need to be immobilized with limited non-weight-bearing activities until it healed—which she had thrown a fit about.

I had been working on her paperwork when I overheard her say that she was by herself for the next two weeks. Usually, I tried to stay out of a patient's business, but I couldn't with Lia. I knew that her stubborn ass would make life miserable for whoever tried to help her, yet I found myself volunteering to be that person.

She had been quiet and sulky the entire ride home, even after I stopped and grabbed us dinner at McDonald's on the way. I had considered getting her a happy meal, just to fuck with her about how childish she was acting, but decided against it when she gave me the death glare I was accustomed to getting at work.

I pulled into the driveway and saw her tense beside me as I gently put the car in park. I got out and went around to help her out, only to have her swat at me like a feral cat.

"Are you seriously going to do this?" I asked, staring down at her as she attempted to swing her good leg out of the car.

"Do what?"

"Be so difficult," I muttered, moving in and helping her get her other leg out without injuring it more.

"I'm not being difficult. I'm just trying to get out of the car so I can go inside and enjoy my dinner. ALONE."

"Yeah, well, good luck with that." I pressed my lips into a thin line to keep from laughing as her icy blue eyes narrowed on me.

"Why? Are you planning to stalk me some more? Should I leave a window open or something to make it easier?" She tilted her head to the side, her brown hair flopping over in the high ponytail she had it in.

"You should be thankful that I even heard you through an open window, Lia. If not, you'd still be shivering on the floor of the shower, unable to get up."

She rolled her eyes but allowed herself to take the hand I offered before I wrapped my arm around her waist and lifted her out of the car. I ignored the way her body felt against mine and slowly moved back until I could get her steady by the side of the car while I grabbed her crutches from the backseat.

"You were just looking for an excuse to burst into my bathroom and see me naked."

I stood in front of her, pulling the crutches back when she reached for them. She started to lose her balance until I stepped directly in front of her, bracing her with my leg in between hers as my chest pressed against her.

"Let's just get one thing clear," I said, my voice suddenly hoarse. "Make no mistake that if I wanted to see you naked, I would go about it the right way. What happened in there earlier wasn't that at all, Lia. And honestly, I couldn't even tell you what you look like naked because I didn't notice. My brain *immediately* went into rescue mode so I could assess your injury and determine the next steps—nothing more."

Her eyes had been locked on mine as I spoke, but I noticed a quick flash of something in them when I said *nothing more*. Before I could identify what it was, she looked away, her features instantly hardening again.

"Do you think you can use these without falling and get yourself inside the house?" I asked, holding the crutches out to her.

"Yes, I'm not stupid. Give them to me."

She reached out for them, only to have me pull them away again.

"If we're going to spend all of our time together for the next few weeks, you're going to have to start using some manners."

It wasn't necessary, but I found that I loved riling her up more than anything. She arched an eyebrow as she looked from me to the house, trying to determine whether she could get inside without them.

"You won't make it," I said softly, standing beside her as she glared at me. "But I have these right here, ready for you to use them. All you have to do is say *one little word*."

She turned the best she could, squared her shoulders, and looked me in the eyes.

"Fuck. You."

"Is that an offer? Cause I'm not going to lie, your foul mouth really does something to me."

"Well, then you'll be impressed to see what I can do with my two bare hands if you don't hand over the crutches?"

I raised my eyebrows and then wiggled them suggestively.

"You mean like a double jacksaw?" I whispered loudly.

She frowned and scrunched her nose up in confusion.

"A what?" She shook her head and closed her eyes. "Never mind. I don't even want to know."

"I don't know, the flush on your cheeks says you might be a bit curious," I teased, enjoying the color washing over her face.

"The only thing I'm curious about is what color your nose will be after I break it."

"Is this because you're hungry? I noticed that at the hospital when you were on my rotation. You'd always get a little more hostile around feeding time."

"Feeding time? Are you comparing me to an animal?"

"If the shoe fits." I shrugged. "Just saying, you could be inside, sitting on the couch, resting your ankle, and enjoying your Big Mac already if you would just stop being so stubborn and say please."

She shifted her weight the best she could and then sighed heavily.

"Fine. May I *please* have the crutches?"

I smiled brightly at her, knowing it pissed her off even more.

"There, that wasn't so hard, was it?"

"You're such an ass," she grumbled as she took them from me and got herself situated.

"Takes one to know one. Let me grab the food real quick, and then I'll unlock the door and help you in."

I made sure she was good before reaching in and grabbing the bag of food and the drink tray, then shut the door with my hip.

"This way," I said, nodding to my house as she started hobbling over to the one she'd been staying at.

"I don't think so." She shook her head.

"Are we doing this the hard way or the easy way?" I asked, pushing the front door open. She continued to glare at me for a few seconds before she turned and started back toward the other house.

I growled in frustration as I set the food and drinks down on the island and then rushed out the door to catch up to her. She was surprisingly good on crutches and I didn't give her enough credit for how fast she could move on them.

"We could have done this the easy way," I said, bending down to scoop her into my arms. The crutches fell to the ground as I caught her off guard, which was nice because then she couldn't swing one at my head and use it as a weapon.

"What are you doing? Put me down!"

"I'm taking care of you, damn it."

"No, you're kidnapping me because you're so obsessed with me that you can't stand the thought of being away from me. You have a sickness, Dr. Dickhead, and you need to get it taken care of."

"The only thing I'm obsessed with is reality cooking shows, which I plan to binge-watch this week while I'm home taking care of you," I panted as I tried to walk through the front door—which would have been easy had Lia not grabbed onto the frame and held on with Hercules strength.

"I'm not staying here with you," she snarled angrily. "Take me to my house, or I'm going to scream at the top of my lungs that you're trying to kidnap me."

"Good luck with that. The closest neighbor is a few blocks away, separated by thick woods. No one will hear you, and if they did, they'd probably turn around and leave you here with me when they see how mean you are."

I finally pushed hard enough to break her grip on the door and sped past anything else she could get a hold of until I reached the couch and deposited her on it.

"Now sit still while I go grab your crutches. If you try to leave, we'll just do this again," I warned, trying to catch my breath.

She folded her arms over her chest and glared at me.

"Are you actually going to listen to me for once?" I asked in disbelief, making sure I had my keys in my pocket in case she dared to get up and try to lock me out while I grabbed her stuff.

"You didn't give me much of a choice." She rolled her eyes and looked away but I could see the tears hiding in them.

I rushed out and grabbed her crutches, then brought them in and sat them on the other couch near her so she could easily reach them if needed. I knew she was hungry, so I got the food and handed her the bag as I turned on the TV to find something to watch. It felt weird having Lia in my house, but the excited energy that ran through me at the thought of taking care of her was something I hadn't expected.

Four
Lia

When Mason said we were going to sit and binge-watch reality cooking shows, he wasn't lying. It had only been two hours, but it felt like more when I found myself completely invested in the show that we had been watching all evening.

"There's no way that's cooked all the way," I scoffed, leaning against the couch and shaking my head as I tried to get comfortable.

"What is she making?" Mason asked as he came back into the living room.

"A pork chop, but she didn't give herself enough time because she was too focused on making her sauce and sides."

"Rookie mistake," he commented as he sat beside me, the same spot he had been sitting in since we got here. There was plenty of seating in his spacious living room, but this was the only couch that directly faced the TV, and I could tell by how worn that seat was that it was where he always sat.

"She's sweating up there. Look at her. You can tell she knows that she just totally screwed herself." I laughed and held the throw pillow tighter against my side as I tried to get comfortable. My body was still achy and sore from the fall earlier, and even though the majority of the impact had happened to my ankle, I had also hurt my side in the process.

"It's almost time for your next pain pill," Mason said, his attention directly on me instead of the TV. It didn't surprise me that he was hyperaware of my discomfort, but it was a bit surprising how easily he could identify the second I started to feel the pain again.

"I'm okay."

"Lia,' he warned with a heavy exhale.

"Dr. Dickhead," I mimicked, the corners of my lips tugging up as I felt his glare on me.

"You should know how important pain management is, Lia. Staying on top of your doses is important for keeping the pain controlled, as well as managing the inflammation. You're not proving anything to anyone by not taking your pills—other than that you're as stubborn as a mule. But we already knew that." His voice was stern and reminded me of the countless times I'd heard it when he was lecturing patients in the ER.

"I don't think the pills are going to help much with *this* pain, but thanks, Doc. My ankle feels fine, so I'll ride it out until I get uncomfortable."

"What kind of pain are you having?" He sat forward and turned to face me, the wheels in his head already turning a mile a minute as his eyes scanned my body, looking for the source.

"I'm fine. Now let's watch her get kicked off for her shitty pork chops." I tried to make light of it, but he was determined and focused, so there was no trying to distract him.

"Lia, show me where it hurts."

I sighed heavily, letting my head fall back against the couch.

"No."

"No?" He got up and sat on the wooden coffee table in front of me, blocking my view of the TV. "What do you mean *no*?"

"I mean I'm not going to show you where it hurts, so leave me alone and stop asking."

His head fell forward on another long sigh as he shoved a hand through his short, dark hair.

"You're going to be the death of me," he muttered, but loud enough that I could hear him.

"Aww!" I squealed. "That's incredible! And here I was, thinking I was going to have to find some way to poison you while watching these cooking shows. You know, undercooked pork was currently in the lead. Just saying."

 "Well, lucky for me, I know better than to eat anything you cook. And I'm safe for a few weeks—at minimum—since you can't be on your feet."

"Where there's a will, there's a way." I gave him a smug smile and went to fold my arms over my chest when I winced at the movement.

"Shirt up. Now," he commanded, leaning forward.

I raised an eyebrow at him in disbelief and stared at him.

"Do it, or I'll do it for you."

"Will you leave me alone if I do?" I asked with venom in my voice.

"For now. Let's go, lift it up."

I made a face at him and then pushed the pillow out of the way so I could grab the bottom of the t-shirt I was wearing. My skin was still hyper-sensitive with the brush of my fingers against it eliciting more pain. I closed my eyes and bit down on my tongue to keep from crying out in pain.

I could feel the air change around me as he leaned in, his fingers feathery light across my skin as he traced the outline of the bruise.

"Did you hit something as you fell?" he asked, my eyes opening to find his locked on mine.

"I don't remember. It all happened so fast that it's kind of a blur. I know I tried to grab onto whatever I could to keep from falling, but once I hurt my ankle, I didn't pay attention to pain anywhere else until now."

"You must've fallen into the edge of the shelf," he answered, his eyes moving back to the bruise on my side. "Can you lift the fabric of your bra so I can see where the bruising stops?"

I nodded and reached around, gently pulling it from my skin and moving it up as high as I could without letting my breast pop free. It made sense that I hit the edge of the shelf since I was injured on the side closest to it. The tile was smooth, but the ledge wasn't, and as I looked down, I noticed scratches from where it had scraped my skin.

"I'm going to get some ointment to put on it. I'll be right back."

He got up and headed toward the back of the house while I tried to get comfortable again. Even though I wasn't thankful for much when it came to Dr. Dickhead, I was thankful he insisted on taking care of me since I didn't have any other options with everyone being out of town.

Five
Lia

By eight o'clock, I was exhausted and ready to go to bed. It had been a long day, and the pain meds Mason insisted I take were making me drowsy. He refused to let me go back to Jones and Bella's house, claiming that I couldn't take care of myself yet. I knew he was right, but that didn't mean I liked his answer.

"I'd be more comfortable there," I whined, knowing it was a losing battle.

"Tough shit," he replied, grabbing a pile of bedding from a linen closet in the hallway and heading into the master bedroom he claimed I would be sleeping in tonight.

"I'm not sleeping in your bed."

"Yes, you are."

"Uh—no, I'm not," I mocked, steadying myself on the crutches. "I know we worked together for six weeks, but that doesn't mean I'm just going to climb into bed with you, Dr. Dickhead."

"I hate to break it to you, Lia, but you have a broken ankle. You can't do shit on your own, including getting in and out of bed. You'll sleep in here because this bed is the lowest to the ground, making it easier for you to get in and out *when* needed. It's also the biggest bedroom in the house so I can put an air mattress on the floor and be here if you need anything."

"You don't know what I can or can't do," I retorted, even though I knew it was stupid. If anything, he knew more about my limitations, having worked in the ER for several years.

"I know more than you think, and you better knock that bratty attitude off before it gets you in trouble."

"Why? What are you going to do? Bend me over your knee and spank me?" I teased, but the look that flashed across his face made tingles immediately snake up my spine.

"You couldn't handle it if I did," he replied quietly as he changed the sheets on the bed and tossed the old ones into a pile on the floor. "I'll run next door and grab your stuff if you tell me what you need."

"No thanks, perv boy. I'm not having you go through my stuff. If the *warden* will let me out of the house, I'll go grab it myself."

He stood up and exhaled heavily as if the weight of the world was sitting on his shoulders.

"Perv boy?" he questioned, one eyebrow cocked. "If you're going to keep coming up with nicknames for me, I'm going to pick some choice ones for you."

"Yeah? Like what?"

"I don't know. Maybe Lia Cocksucker. That has a nice ring to it, doesn't it?"

"Not in the least. At least Dr. Dickhead is somewhat close to Doctor Dickson. Cocksucker is not even close to Capshaw."

He shrugged and gave me a smug smile.

"What do you need from next door?" he pressed, grabbing the dirty linens from the floor and tossing them in the hamper in the walk-in closet.

"I told you, I'll go get it myself."

"Why are you being so difficult?"

"Why are *you?* I have crutches—in case you didn't notice. I can easily walk next door, grab what I need, and be back before lockdown happens."

"You do realize that *next door* isn't as close as it seems, right? It's a bit of a distance between the two houses, which means it's even more of a trek for someone with a *broken* ankle."

"Whatever," I said with a sigh of resignation. "How about I rest tonight, and then when I'm feeling better tomorrow, I'll go home."

"You're with me for two weeks, Lia. Just accept it. However, I will concede on letting you go get your stuff tomorrow. Do you need something to sleep in tonight?"

"I'm good in what I have," I answered, not wanting to get into another fight about my staying with him for a prolonged period of time.

He helped me into bed and handed me my phone before heading back to the living room to get something. I was about to put it on the charger when I noticed a new text message. I opened the screen and smiled when I saw a group text message from Kensy and Bella.

Bella: I'm just checking in to see how things are going.

Kensy: We're good, just getting ready to go to dinner. How are things going, Lia?

The text messages came in ten minutes ago, so thankfully, no one had freaked out about me not texting back right away. They probably assumed I was already drunk off margaritas and ice cream and called it a night.

Me: Things are fine, but I kinda fell and broke my ankle this morning.

I stared at the phone for a few minutes as I heard Mason rummaging around in the linen closet again.

Bella: OH MY GOD! Are you okay?

Bella: Let me check the next flights home and see how quickly I can get there.

Kensy: LIA! Are you okay? What happened?

Kensy: Your brother said we can leave tonight and get back by morning.

Me: STOP.

Me: I'm fine—thank you both for your concern. No one needs to come home.

Me: I slipped on some shampoo in the shower this morning and twisted my ankle, resulting in a minor break. I don't have to have surgery, but I am stuck in a cast for a month or two until it heals.

Bella: It sounds like you need help, Lia. How are you going to do stuff if you're in a cast?

Kensy: I agree. You need someone to be there to take care of you. We're checking flights now.

Me: I'm at Mason's house.

Kensy: Who?

Bella: Yeah, who?

Me: Dr. Dickhead

Before I could type anything else, my phone began ringing, Kensy's name appearing on the screen.

"Hey," I said, swiping my finger across the screen to answer it. "I'm fine. You guys don't need to keep worrying."

"You fell and broke your ankle, and now you're staying with someone you talk about hating all the time. That doesn't sound fine to me," Bella said. Apparently, we were on a three-way call.

"I was calling for help, and he heard me through the bathroom window. I had cracked it to keep it from getting steamy. Also—why didn't you mention before that he was Jones's next-door neighbor?" I hissed, hoping he didn't walk in right now.

"We thought about telling you but knew you wouldn't move in if you knew he lived there," Bella answered softly.

"Well, you would have been right about that." I shifted against the pillows, envious of how soft and fluffy they were compared to the ones I used at home.

"Are you sure you're okay?" Kensy asked. "We don't mind coming home early. You can come stay with us."

"I'm okay. Really. It's been a long day, and I'm exhausted, but Mason insisted that I stay with him for a few weeks."

"A few weeks?" Kensy and Bella asked in disbelief at the same time.

"You're okay with that?" Kensy probed.

"I don't know. I guess. I mean, it can't really get any worse than it is. I fell and broke my ankle. He saw me naked. Now he's helping to take care of me, so I guess things are fine."

"WHO THE FUCK SAW HER NAKED?" my brother growled from the background.

"No one," Kensy assured him. "Now be quiet so I can hear as she tells me all the juicy details."

I grinned, already picturing the scowl on his face as she tormented him.

"There are no juicy details. I was only naked because I had been in the shower. He practically threw a towel at me right away so he didn't have to see me naked," I whispered so Mason wouldn't hear me. "There's nothing going on between us whatsoever. He's just taking care of me because he feels obligated to. As soon as I can be more self-sufficient, I'll be on my own and out of his hair."

"I don't like you being there by yourself, even if he's helping to take care of you," Bella said warily. "I would feel better if one of us came back instead."

"She's fine and in perfect hands with Mason," Jones chimed in.

"Am I on everyone's speakerphone?" I asked, feeling somewhat self-conscious.

"Sorry, I knew that Jones would have questions as soon as I hung up, so I thought it would be easier to just put the call on speakerphone. That way, I didn't have to repeat everything," Bella explained.

"Same for me," Kensy added. "You know your brother will have a million and one questions; this just cuts down on the amount I have to answer."

"Fair enough." I sighed, the exhaustion catching up to me again. "Thank you guys for checking in on me, but I'm fine. Really."

"Well, you are shacked up with the town's best ER doctor. Can't really do any better than that," Kensy said cheerfully. "Plus, hot, angry hate sex can be reallllly good. Just wait and see."

"She's not seeing anything," my brother cut in. "And if he touches her, he won't be seeing shit either."

Just then, Mason walked into the room with a knowing smirk as he tossed the air mattress on the floor.

"I gotta go. I'll talk to you guys tomorrow." I hung up and looked away as a blush covered my skin at the thought that Kensy could be right about some hot hate sex.

34

<u>Six</u>
Mason

Plus, hot, angry hate sex can be reallllly good. Just wait and see.

I hadn't been able to stop thinking about the look on Lia's face when I walked into the room and interrupted her phone call before she promptly hung up and tried to hide her blush from me. I got myself situated on the air mattress and set the alarm on my phone for three hours so I could give her the next pain pill while she rustled around on the bed, trying to get comfortable.

"Do you need anything?" I asked, setting my phone down beside me and making sure it was charging.

"Can you take this stupid cast off? I don't know how anyone sleeps with this stupid thing on."

"Unfortunately, no. But I can try to adjust the pillow it's propped up on," I offered, sitting up to find her looking guilty as her leg was flat on the bed.

I closed my eyes, sighed, and let out a growl.

"You're the most infuriating woman. You know that, right?"

I got up, walked over to the bed, and stared down at her with my most intimidating doctor glare. Usually, it worked for other patients, but not Lia. No, she just batted her beautiful eyes and acted like she didn't know why I was upset.

"You need to keep your leg elevated above your heart, Lia. You know that."

"Yeah, but it hurts my thigh all the way up to my ass."

"*You're* a pain in *my* ass," I grumbled, grabbing the pillows and waiting for her to lift her leg so I could rearrange them.

"I told you to take me home, but *noooo.* Dr. Dickhead had to be the knight in shining armor, swooping in to rescue the poor damsel in distress. Spoiler alert—I don't need saving. Just let me go back to my house, and you won't have to worry about me being a pain in your ass anymore."

"Nice try. You and I both know that you aren't able to take care of yourself right now, yet you find some pleasure in making things hard for me."

My cheeks burned the second embarrassment washed over me when I realized the words I had just said. I didn't mean it *that* way, but the flush on her face confirmed she'd heard it the same way.

"Not something most guys would complain about," she whispered with a hint of humor in her tone.

"Yeah, well, I'm not most guys. Lift your leg."

She rolled her eyes but did as I asked, using both hands to hold it as I slid the pillows in underneath it. I knew there was a chance she would try to kick them out from beneath her in her sleep, but for now, it would have to work.

"Happy?" she asked, folding her arms over her chest.

I arched an eyebrow at her but said nothing. It was getting late, and it had already been a long day, so I didn't want to drag things out by fighting with her. We had at least two weeks to torment each other, so some of it could wait until morning when Lia got a fresh dose of feistiness.

I walked over and grabbed my phone from the charger on the floor, then picked up my pillow and walked over to the other side of the bed.

"I am now," I said as I climbed in beside her and set my phone on the wireless charger on the nightstand.

"What are you doing?" she shrieked, sitting up as much as she could and pulling the sheet over her chest. She looked cute, all wide-eyed and panicked.

"Going to sleep. You should get some rest, too."

"Ummm—why are you in the bed? I thought you said you were going to sleep on the air mattress?"

"I did. But then you decided to be difficult and kick the pillows out from beneath your leg, so now I'm forced to sleep beside you to make sure you don't do that again."

"What?" She let out a semi-hysterical laugh as she stared at me in disbelief. "Okay, okay, point made. I won't do it again. Now you can go back to your air mattress and leave me be."

"Yeah, it doesn't really work that way, Lia."

"What do you mean? Why not?"

"I don't trust you anymore. You've proven that you don't have the desire to take care of yourself; therefore, you've pushed me into a position where I have to watch over you more closely. I'm concerned about your well-being, which means we're bed buddies from here on."

"Bed buddies? What the hell are bed buddies?"

"Us. You and me. Two grown adults who will be sharing a bed. And if you get so much as even an inkling to do something while I sleep—I can guarantee you'll pay for it in the morning. Now close your eyes and your mouth and go to sleep. I'll get you up at midnight for your next pain pill."

"Mason, you can't be serious," she objected, her jaw still hanging open.

"Goodnight, Lia."

I rolled onto my side and didn't try to fight the smirk that spread across my face. Thankfully, I was a light sleeper—just in case Lia tried to kill me in my sleep.

<u>Seven</u>
Lia

Mason is an asshole. There—I said it. It wasn't like it was surprising news to me, given how much he'd made my blood boil while I did my six-week rotation with him. But Mason outside of work was more infuriating—if that was even possible.

By the time I'd finally gotten comfortable enough to fall asleep last night, he was waking me up to take a stupid pain pill. As if listening to him snore for two hours wasn't bad enough, he was one of those people who could *immediately* go back to sleep as soon as they laid their heads down. I *hated* people like that. Once I was awake, it took at least an hour for me to fall back asleep, which meant that I was only getting an hour of sleep—tops—every time he woke me up. Sometimes, it was to get me to take a pain pill, other times, it was because he insisted that my leg wasn't properly propped up on the pillow and needed to be adjusted. If I had the strength, I would have adjusted his neck so I wouldn't have to deal with him anymore.

The sun leaked through the sheer curtains, casting a warm glow on the room. I groaned and opened one eye, looking for Mason and finding relief when he wasn't in bed beside me. I heard the shower running and relaxed, hoping he would be in there for a while.

I sat up the best I could and reached over for my crutches, cursing under my breath as I almost fell out of bed trying to get them.

"Stupid fucking crutches," I hissed, pulling the pillows out from beneath me so I could turn and put my legs down.

The water was still on, so I moved as quickly as I could, pushing myself with what little strength I had. I closed my eyes and winced as pain radiated through my leg as I lowered my casted foot to the floor. I didn't know when I was due for another pain pill, but I would imagine I was getting close as the fire burned through my leg.

I grabbed the side of the nightstand and lifted myself onto my good foot, keeping my balance as I reached for the crutches and propped them under my arms.

My breath flowed out heavily as I took a moment to catch my bearings. If I moved quickly enough, I could be out of Mason's house and into Jones' before Mason finished his shower. Just then, I heard the water turn off and panicked. I grabbed my phone, holding it between my teeth since I didn't have pockets, and started hopping as fast as I could.

I didn't want to risk slipping and falling, but I knew I had to get out of there. I couldn't spend one more day with Mason, especially with how grumpy I was from the lack of sleep I got last night. It was better for everyone—mainly him—if I went home. I wasn't trying to be difficult, I just had his best interests in mind.

I was halfway down the hall when I heard the bathroom door open. I held my breath and moved faster, trying not to laugh at how ridiculous I must look.

Just as I got to the living room, I heard heavy footsteps behind me.

"Where do you think you're going?" he asked, his voice annoyingly silky smooth behind me.

My skin prickled as he approached, my body reacting to his in a way I hated.

"I was going to make a pot of coffee," I lied, refusing to look at him.

I was closer to the front door than I was to the kitchen, which made it even more unrealistic.

"Is that so?"

"Mmm hmm." I turned my head to avoid looking at him as he stepped around in front of me.

"Well, please, don't let me stop you."

I could hear the mocking tone in his voice as the anger rushed through me.

"You know what?" I asked, semi-snarling.

"What?"

"Go fuck yourself."

"Wow. You're really not a morning person, are you?"

"Not mornings spent around you."

"I think some fried eggs will fix that. Go sit down, and I'll make breakfast," he said dismissively as if I *hadn't* just insulted him.

"I don't think so. I've had enough. I'm going home." I took a deep breath and went to move when he stepped forward, invading my space again.

"We've been through this already, Lia. You're not going home. Now go sit your stubborn ass on the couch and wait for breakfast."

"You're not the boss of me. You do know that, right?"

"That's where you're wrong. I am very much the boss of you and you'll do as I say."

"Or what?" I cocked my head to the side, frustrated that I couldn't plant my hand on my hip without toppling over. *Stupid crutches*.

"Or you'll find that things are a lot harder for you than they need to be. I'm a fairly patient man, Lia, but you keep pushing me and you're going to see a side of me you don't like."

"Oh, Dr. Dickhead," I said with a heavy sigh, shaking my head emphatically. "You really think I like you to begin with?"

He worked his jaw back and forth as he debated on saying anything.

"Go sit on the couch. Now." He pinned me with a look and folded his arms over his broad chest.

I rolled my eyes and stuck my tongue out at him before turning the best I could and hopping over to the couch. I picked up the remote and turned on the TV to ignore the sounds of him moving around in the kitchen. It was going to be a very long two weeks if I was stuck here with him. But just because one escape attempt was foiled didn't mean I wouldn't try again later.

Eight

Mason

"How's your food?" I asked, surprised that Lia had already scarfed half her plate as she shoveled another forkful of food into her mouth.

"It's edible," she said with that same catty tone she'd had all morning. One thing was super clear—she was *not* a morning person.

"Well, if you're eating like *that* and calling it *edible,* then I guess you're one of those women who would fare well in prison."

She turned and glared at me but instead of it pissing me off, it just made her look even cuter.

"If I'm in prison, then it likely means I murdered you, and in that case, I would say it was well worth it. Plus, I'm sure prison food would be better than this."

I rubbed my lips together as I watched her, enjoying the way she used her toast to wipe up the yolk that had run on her plate. She didn't tell me how she wanted her eggs, but I'd spent plenty of time around Lia at the hospital to know. Still, it would have been nice for her to acknowledge that I knew so much about her and what she liked.

I picked up the remote and changed the channel, finding a different cooking show to watch. It wasn't that I didn't enjoy seeing kids try their hand at cooking, but I couldn't stand it when they cried after something didn't turn out how it should. Sad kids was one of the few things that really got to me and pulled at my heartstrings.

"Do you want more?" I asked, nodding to her now empty plate as she chewed.

She shook her head and covered her mouth before she spoke.

"No, thank you."

My eyebrows shot up in surprise as I turned my head and looked at her.

"What?" she asked, clearly annoyed again already.

"Nothing. I just don't think I've ever heard you say those words before."

She rolled her eyes and set her plate on the coffee table, ignoring my comment. Letting well enough be, I got up and took our dishes to the dishwasher. It was going to be a long two weeks with Lia if she kept up this whole *I hate you* attitude, but I didn't know how to make her any less angry. Maybe she really did hate me, but deep down, I felt like perhaps it was just an act she put on.

We sat and watched TV for an hour before I got her next pain pill and handed it to her. I was surprised when she didn't fight me on it, she just took it.

"Do you want me to help you shower today?" I offered, setting her glass of water on the coffee table.

The surprise on her face caught me off guard, making me realize how it must have come across.

"I didn't mean…" I let out a long breath and scrubbed my hands down my face. "I'm sorry; I didn't mean for that to come out the way it did. I just thought maybe you wanted to clean up."

"Do I stink?" she asked, clearly appalled as she lifted her shirt and sniffed it.

"No. God, no. That's not what I was insinuating at all."

"I smell like the hospital." She scrunched her nose.

I wasn't sure what the hospital smelled like to her, but I hadn't noticed anything different. Clearly, she was on a whole other page as she continued sniffing herself and making faces.

"You don't smell, Lia. I was just offering because I know I always feel better after a shower. At some point, you'll need to take one and won't be able to do it on your own, so I'll be helping you with it one way or another. It was just an offer."

"Okay." She nodded her head and inhaled sharply. "You're right. I think I would feel better after a shower. But do you think I can go home and grab some of my stuff so at least I can be comfortable in my own clothes?"

"Yeah. Sure."

I ignored the nagging feeling in the pit of my stomach as I agreed to it. Lia wasn't ever *this* nice to me, which should have been the first clue she was up to something.

Nine
Lia

Mason was obnoxiously close to me as I turned the key in the lock and pushed open the door at Jones's house. He had insisted on coming with me in case I needed any assistance. It was nice, but little did he know that I wasn't planning on getting anything because I wasn't planning on leaving.

"Do you mind checking the mail for me?" I asked, looking over my shoulder as I hopped into the house. "I'm waiting for a check and need to get it deposited as soon as it comes in."

He nodded, not noticing the way my voice changed as the lie rolled off my lips. While I would love to have money waiting for me in my mailbox, the most that would be in there would be junk mail and a stack of coupons to Surf 'N Shack.

"Sure." He took the keys and went outside, leaving me alone long enough for me to hobble over and lock the door. I was beyond pleased with myself as I slid the chain lock into place before stepping back and grinning at my success.

I turned and headed for the couch when I heard the key in the lock.

"Really, Lia?" he growled from outside.

"I'm fine. Go away and leave me alone," I yelled back.

"Not going to happen, and you know it."

"Yeah, well, I already locked the deadbolt and chain lock, so you're going to have a hell of a time trying to get in. Good luck with that, Dr. Dickhead." I leaned back on the soft cushion and closed my eyes as the smug grin pinched my cheeks.

I was surprised by how quickly he gave up, but it didn't matter as long as he let me be. It was so quiet in the house that I could close my eyes and fall asleep—which I desperately wanted right now. This was where I wanted to be. Even though it wasn't technically *my house,* it felt more like home than anything else right now.

My breathing slowed and evened out as my eyes fluttered closed. I was drifting off to sleep when I heard the back door whoosh open. My eyes widened as I stared at Mason, his face tight with frustration as he held the key in the air and smirked.

Fuck. I forgot about the back door.

"Okay, so you got in the house. Doesn't mean I'm going anywhere." I shrugged my shoulders and stared defiantly at him.

He hung his head and shook it.

"Fine. You win."

"What?" I asked in disbelief, leaning forward to hear him better.

"You win, Lia. If this is where you want to stay, then fine."

"Really?"

He nodded, his eyes locked on mine.

"Yeah."

"Just like that? What happened to the whole *I am the boss of you and you'll do what I say?*" I questioned, lowering my voice and shaking my finger as I mocked him.

"Oh, that all still applies."

I frowned as I tried to keep up with him.

"How so? If I'm staying here, you can't force me to do anything if you're not here."

"That's where you're wrong."

Before I could ask what he meant, he turned and walked out the door, taking the only set of keys I had to the house with him.

Fifth Wheel

Ten
Mason

"What on earth are you doing?" Lia exclaimed, nearly jumping off the couch when I opened the door and stepped inside. I shifted to get my duffle bag back to my side while keeping from dropping my pillow.

"If you're staying here, so am I."

"You can't be serious." Her eyes danced wildly as she watched me shut the door and lock it.

"Dead serious," I replied, heading through the living room as she focused on my every move. "Which room is yours?"

"No—this is not happening," she insisted, trying to get up from the couch.

"Don't worry, I'll find it myself. I'm sure it's painted black and has pictures of sad cats taped to the walls."

"You're such an asshole," she called after me as I made my way down the hallway and started peeking into the rooms.

One was a gym, which was impressive but not helpful at the moment. There was a master bedroom at the back of the house, which I assumed was Jones and Bella's room. That left one last room open, the one directly across from the bathroom.

I stepped inside and flipped the lights on, impressed with how neat and organized it was. I could definitely tell it was Lia's room based on the feel of it, but I was still caught off guard by the pink lace bra hanging from the bedpost.

"See something you like?" she asked, leaning on her crutches as she hung out in the doorway.

I looked away from the bra and turned to her.

"You seem to be getting used to the crutches," I commented, ignoring her question.

"Yeah, it's a good skill to have when I need to run away."

"Well, I think we've both seen how well that works out for you." I dropped my duffle bag to the floor out of the way.

"Okay, obviously, I can't stop you from being here, but I can stop you from sleeping in here. This is my space, Mason. Not yours. You need to abide by *my* rules."

"When you can start taking care of yourself, I'll gladly step back, Lia. But you're late on your next pain pill, you haven't bothered to elevate your leg, and you need sleep. So until you can be a functioning adult, I'm here to take care of you—like it or not."

She shook her head and blew out a long breath.

"You're so fucking infuriating."

"Do you know what's even more infuriating?" I asked, stepping in front of her so she had to look at me. "That you keep fighting me on every single thing. I'm trying to be a nice guy here, Lia. You don't have anyone else here to help you, and whether you want to admit it or not—you need help. So stop with this attitude already and just accept it."

She jutted out her chin and narrowed her eyes at me.

"I still think this is just your way of continuing to stalk me."

"Trust me, after the first forty-eight hours with you, I'll be taking a much-needed break the second I can."

I turned and grabbed my duffle bag, looking for my earbuds as she stood there glaring at me from the doorway.

"Grab whatever clothes you want to wear today," I said over my shoulder. "Your ass is taking a shower."

<u>Eleven</u>
Lia

By the time Mason finished wrapping the cast in a trash bag and securing it with medical tape, I was too tired to actually shower. He found a folding chair in the garage and was able to sit it in the walk-in shower so I could sit and wash my hair.

At first, the thought of allowing Mason to see me naked had me crawling out of my skin with anxiety, but he had this way of making it seem like it was no big deal that instantly calmed me. He offered to help with washing my hair and stuck to keeping my leg as far out of the water as possible while also giving me as much privacy as he could. When it came time to wash my body, I focused on the parts I could while sitting, then accepted his help as I stood to wash the rest.

Once I was done, he helped wrap me in a towel before assisting me with getting dressed. We sat down on the couch and flipped through channels on the TV, looking for something to watch as my eyes grew heavier. I leaned to the side, not caring about the pressure I was putting on my bruised ribs. This was the most comfortable I had been since I broke my ankle, and I wasn't going to worry about a bit of pain right now.

I closed my eyes and allowed my body to sink further into the couch, sleep taking me deep into its arms.

****

The smell of bacon pulled me out of my sleep as my stomach growled loudly. I tried to lift myself and then looked down to find my ankle elevated on a stack of pillows on the couch with another pillow tucked under my head. My favorite throw blanket was covering me and I wondered how Mason did all of this without me knowing. I must have been in a deep sleep and dead to the world.

"Perfect timing," he said from the kitchen, somehow knowing I was awake.

"How do you do that?" I asked, pushing myself up.

"Do what?"

"Know the second I'm awake. It's creepy."

"The sweet sound of you *not* snoring anymore," he replied with a laugh.

"I do not snore," I countered, turning to look at him over the back of the couch.

"You do. You're quite the noisy sleeper."

"I disagree. I'm as quiet as a mouse."

"A flatulent mouse."

My cheeks reddened immediately at the thought that I possibly farted in my sleep, and Mason heard it.

I lowered my head against the cushion to shield myself from being seen.

"Don't worry about it. We all do it," he assured as he came around and handed me a plate.

"That makes me worry more." I took the food from him and pulled myself into the best upright position I could. He sat down in the chair across from me and turned on the TV.

"What did you do while I was sleeping?" I asked, realizing how quiet the house had been.

"I took advantage of using the gym equipment in the other room and listened to a podcast." He pointed to the earbuds sitting on the coffee table.

"You don't have to do this, you know?" I said, looking down at my plate. "I know you're just being kind because I don't have anyone else, but I don't want to be a burden to you. I can figure out how to do this on my own."

He lifted his sandwich to his mouth and took a bite. I tried to ignore the way his jaw looked as he chewed, his features slowly growing on me as I realized how attractive he really was.

"You're not a burden," he replied slowly after swallowing his bite. "You could make things easier by not fighting me on everything, but you're not a burden."

"I feel like I am. You're taking off time from work to stay home and take care of someone who is mean to you every chance they get."

"I have a lot of PTO. It's not a big deal."

"Yeah, but most people would go take a vacation. Go somewhere tropical. Lie on a beach drinking fruity frozen drinks. Not stay in town and care for their grumpy next-door neighbor."

"Well, you know you could try *not* being mean to me. That might be a nice change."

"What fun would that be?" I said with a snort, picking my sandwich up and examining it without spilling the chips.

"It's a BLT minus the mayo," he answered.

"How did you know I don't like mayo?"

"I know more than you think I do."

He got up and took his empty plate to the sink while I took my first bite. The taste was amazing for something so simple, but BLTs were my go-to sandwich. I was picky about how I liked them—no mayo, tomato thinly sliced, and bacon crispy. Everything that Mason did without me having to ask.

Twelve

Mason

We almost made it one whole day without Lia trying to kill me.

Okay, so she didn't *technically* try to kill me, but she decided to put on the world's smallest booty shorts after her shower. It wouldn't have been bad other than her constantly trying to get comfortable on the couch and shifting into positions that pulled them tightly across her ass which was barely covered by the thin fabric. I would have said it was innocent and she was just wearing whatever was most comfortable, but when she paired it with a tight tank top and smirked, I knew she was trying to kill me.

After lunch, Lia took another nap, which gave me some time to figure out what to make for dinner based on the groceries in the fridge. Lia had insisted that she had bought healthy food when she went grocery shopping yesterday, but the cartons of ice cream and frozen pizzas said otherwise. There was a mismatch of healthy foods, from a few cucumbers to an eggplant—both of which I didn't question what her intention was with them. But nothing to make a salad like she insisted she wanted.

While she was snoring loudly, I snuck over to my house and grabbed the produce I had, not sure what kind of salad Lia was wanting. It was hard to get anything out of her— other than sarcasm—so I was on my own to figure things out for the next few weeks. I knew that she wasn't going to just give in and accept my help, but I also wasn't going to leave her to try to do stuff on her own. While she was doing better at getting around on her crutches, there was still a lot she couldn't easily do, and I felt better knowing I was there to help when needed.

Jones had texted me this morning to see if they needed to come home but I assured him I was fine with Lia. It was nice of them to worry about her so much, but I was already there and willing to help out, so I didn't see a reason for them to cut their honeymoon short.

When I got back to the house, Lia was still sleeping, which I was happy about. I knew she had slept like shit last night and anticipated she would have another hard night tonight. At least her body was getting the rest it needed now. I wasn't sure if it was because she was in more pain and had more discomfort at night or if it was because I had been in the same bed as her, but tonight wasn't going to be any different. Something about being next to her as she slept made me feel better, knowing that I could easily check on her when I needed to.

I had finished washing and cutting the veggies when Lia finally woke up.

"What are you doing?" she asked groggily, pushing herself up on the couch.

I turned to look at her and then immediately turned back around when I noticed her boob had popped out of the side of her tank top while she was sleeping. The sports bra she had on underneath covered her skin, but still, it was just sitting there in the open.

"Working on stuff for the salad for dinner," I replied loud enough for my voice to carry since I wasn't looking at her.

"You didn't have to do that. Just because I wanted to eat healthy food doesn't mean you have to."

"I eat healthy food all the time. However, I didn't know what kind of salad you were planning to make, given all you had was an eggplant and a few cucumbers."

I heard her moving around behind me and then turned to make sure she was okay. Thankfully her boob had been put back in its place and was no longer out as she hobbled over on her crutches.

"I was planning to make eggplant parmigiana for dinner this week," she explained. "I figured it was healthier than the chicken parmigiana I really wanted. I bought the cucumbers because I like eating cucumber sandwiches. They didn't have much for salad while I was at the store so I was planning to order in tonight. Where did all of this come from?" she asked, leaning in next to me, her arm brushing against mine.

"I ran home and grabbed stuff while you were sleeping. I had fresh produce and figured we could start there. Where were you ordering a salad from?"

Her cheeks flushed the most adorable shade of pink when she looked up at me.

"Tipsy Taquito."

I frowned, trying to remember their menu. Mostly everything they had there was fried.

"Do they have salads there?"

She nodded and shifted her weight on the crutches.

"My friend Bella always gets salads when we go."

"Oh, I don't think I've ever noticed them on the menu."

"Well, I guess it's not technically a *salad*," she said with a soft laugh I didn't hear often enough. "It's their taco salad. She gets it without the shell, which makes it healthier."

"Is that what you were getting?"

She nodded her head, but I could read the lie on her face.

"So what you're saying is you really wanted a taco salad for dinner tonight, not actual salad?"

"This looks good, too," she insisted with a giggle.

I looked down at the cutting board filled with carrots, cucumbers, tomatoes, olives, and red onions and then looked up at her.

"We can save these for a snack tray tomorrow," I said, pulling my shoulders back and turning to look at her. "If you really want a taco salad tonight, I can run and pick up dinner."

"You don't have to do that, Mason. This is fine. Really."

"You're a terrible liar. Things will work a lot easier if you tell me what you want. Don't tell me what you think I want to hear because that just makes more work for both of us."

"I've told you so many times already that you don't have to keep taking care of me. I'm fine on my own. I can order dinner in and sleep on the couch tonight. I seem to do well there, and it's surprisingly comfortable." She turned and rested her back against the counter, already looking ready to run back to the couch.

I moved in front of her, pinning her against the counter as I pressed my leg in between hers without bumping her cast. She tried to look away until I lifted her chin with my finger and forced her to look at me.

"You can try to get rid of me all you want, but I'm not going anywhere, Lia. Face it, you're stuck with me for the next two weeks. Like I said before, we can either do this the easy way or we can keep doing it the hard way. The choice is yours."

My body was so close to hers that I could feel the heat coming off of hers as well as the rise and fall of her chest as she sucked in a shuddered breath at my words. The close proximity was enough to send a jolt of electricity through me, straight to my cock which immediately hardened in my jeans. I didn't have to question whether or not she felt it because the small gasp that escaped between her pursed lips confirmed it.

"Like I said, Lia, the choice is yours. Tell me what you want for dinner, and I'll put the order in."

I pushed away from her and walked outside, needing some fresh air to cool me off before I did something stupid—like kiss her.

Thirteen
Lia

What the fuck was that?

My breathing was quick and heavy as my mind scrambled to process what had just happened with Mason. Did he literally pin me against the counter again? Why was that so hot, and why did I like it so much when he forced me to look at him?

I'd read about these kind of things in steamy romance novels but always thought it was borderline cheesy with how quickly the girls would react and be ready to jump the guy's bones, but here I was—practically panting and ready to throw my crutches to the wind and hump the guy I hated.

It hadn't even been a full forty-eight hours with Mason yet, and I was already ready to bang him. What the hell was that? Never in my life had I ever entertained sexual thoughts about him until now—which was incredibly unsettling. I didn't have feelings for him other than violence-driven ones that would result in some sort of attempted murder. But yet that didn't seem to settle the aching that was starting to build between my thighs.

I grabbed my crutches and hopped over to the couch, needing a moment to rest before letting my thoughts spiral out of control. My stomach growled, reminding me that I was hungry and probably just needed food. Yeah, that was all I needed—some nice, thick, hard cock. Food. I needed FOOD.

I shook my head, the frustration building quickly as I hated where my thoughts kept going. Just because I'd felt him against me didn't mean that I needed to fuck him. It also didn't mean that I didn't want to, but that was just because I was going through a dry spell, and girls have needs. I just needed a killer orgasm, and then I could go back to hating him.

Not like I could ask him to help with that, but I could take him up on grabbing us dinner and take care of myself while he was gone. It was clear he wasn't going to leave me alone more than necessary, so this was the only chance I was going to get.

I took a deep breath and slowly let it out, my mind already made up with a plan of action when he came back inside. He looked at me and then looked away, a slight flush still on his cheeks. Obviously, it had impacted him as much as it had me, which was strange since I was pretty sure he hated me as much as I hated him—even if he was taking care of me. But that wasn't because he liked me; that was because he felt compelled as a doctor to take care of the pathetic woman who had no one else.

"Did you decide what you want?" he asked, sitting down in the chair across from me.

My eyes widened, wondering how he knew what I was planning.

"Excuse me?"

His brow furrowed as he looked at me, confused.

"For dinner. Did you decide what you wanted so I can go pick it up?"

"Oh!" I shook my head quickly and refocused myself. "Yes, I'll do the taco salad, please. No onion or sour cream, extra shredded cheese, and pico de gallo on the side. If you don't mind grabbing my purse, I'll give you cash."

"Don't worry about it, I got it. Do you want anything else?"

"Would you mind getting a side of chips and queso?"

"No problem." He stood up and gave me a quick once-over. "Do you need anything before I go?"

"Nope. I'm good, but thanks."

He hesitated for a moment before grabbing the keys off the counter and locking the door behind him. I let out a heavy sigh, grabbed my crutches, and headed toward the bedroom. Tipsy Taquito wasn't that far, and I moved a lot slower than usual, so if I wanted a few minutes to take care of myself, I needed to move as quickly as possible.

Once I got to the bedroom, I didn't bother closing the door. It was way too much work, and I had one mission—to come. Plus, it would just be more time when the clock was already working against me. I had definitely underestimated the time it would take to get to the bedroom, to begin with, which made me nervous that Mason might be back before I was done. Hopefully they would be busy at Tipsy Taquito to buy me a few more minutes.

I walked to the side of the bed and pulled my vibrating rose out of the drawer, frowning when I tried to turn it on and it wouldn't. I had meant to charge it yesterday, but then the day got completely off track with me breaking my ankle.

I frowned and grabbed the small bullet-looking one Bella had gotten me for my birthday from Dark Vibes. It wasn't my favorite, but it would do the job.

I sat down on the edge of the bed and carefully laid my crutches along the bottom so I could reach them easily once I was done. My body was tense and on high alert as I struggled to get comfortable on the bed without hurting myself. The cast felt like it weighed at least twenty pounds, and by the time I got situated, I was panting and out of breath. I laid back on the pillows and allowed myself a few minutes to rest and catch my breath. I grabbed my phone and went to my favorite porn site, scrolling through the videos but realizing I was pretty much still ready to go. Mason had barely touched me, yet I was still wet and aching for a release from the few thoughts I'd allowed myself to entertain.

A video of a girl giving head to one guy while getting pounded from behind by another caught my attention. I clicked into it and turned down the sound. I didn't need to hear the cheesy lines they were saying to get me off. I much preferred to make up my own dialogue and imagined what I thought they would be saying instead.

My hand roamed over my breast, brushing across my nipples as they hardened beneath the fabric of my bra. I pulled the cup down, allowing the cold air from the air conditioner to stiffen it further before gently tugging it between my fingers.

The guy in the video pulled out of her and then slammed back in, gripping her hips as he held her in place and plowed into her. I let my legs fall to the sides as I watched, getting wetter by the second.

I turned the bullet on and moved my shorts and panties to the side before pressing the bullet against my clit. I closed my eyes and arched my back as I got used to the intense vibration. My hips rocked as I tried to find the right rhythm that I needed as I turned up the sound to try to get me there quicker. At this point, I was desperate to come, and the sounds of others might have been enough to get me there. If my rose were working, I would already be done and riding a cloud of ecstasy. But the bullet always took longer to do the trick, which was why it wasn't my favorite.

I shifted again, making sure I didn't fall off the side of the bed, and pressed it harder against my clit and rubbed.

"Hey, dinner is—"

"OH MY GOD!" I screamed, my eyes flying open to find Mason standing in the doorway. Without thinking, I panicked and threw the bullet at him, hitting him smack in the middle of his forehead.

Fourteen
Mason

"Ouch," I said, rubbing the spot on my forehead where something hit me. I was still trying to figure out what was going on when I heard a buzzing noise. I bent down and picked up a pink bullet-looking toy, my eyes widening immediately as I realized what it was.

Lia scrambled on the bed, yanking her top up and fixing her shorts as her cheeks flushed seven shades of red.

"What are you doing in here?" she shrieked, bringing my attention back to the situation at hand.

"Um," I said, clearing my throat. "Dinner is here. I'm sorry; I shouldn't have just barged in on you. I honestly didn't stop to think that you might be…."

I paused and swallowed hard past the dryness in my throat as I continued to hold the sex toy in my hand. I looked down at it, my curiosity getting the better of me as I pressed the button to turn it off.

"I'm sorry—I have to ask," I said with a chuckle as I held it up. "What the hell is this?"

"Nothing," she snapped, struggling to grab her crutches and get off the bed.

"I mean, obviously, it's a vibrator, but why is it so small? It's like a micro penis. It's so small and thin." I held it in front of me, twisting and turning it to get a better look. "Does this actually do anything?"

"I'm not answering that, as it's none of your business."

"I mean, it kind of is, given that you hit me in the head with it." I reached up and rubbed the spot it had hit. "I mean, what if I have a tiny dick-sized bruise on my head tomorrow? How am I going to explain that?"

"Sounds like a *you* problem," she said, hopping in front of me and holding her hand out.

I handed it to her but couldn't keep the smirk off my lips.

"I still have so many questions about this," I teased.

"Yeah, well, you're never going to get answers to them." She turned and hopped over to the nightstand before opening a drawer and tossing the toy inside.

"Sure I will. Eventually, you'll give in and tell me why you like such small dicks."

Her head whipped up as she gave me an ice-cold stare.

"Who said I do?"

"Well, I'm not usually one to say that size matters, but in this case, it does. I mean, come on, Lia, that thing is barely an inch thick—if that. And it's all of like three inches long. I just don't see how it's going to do anything. It's *soo* small."

I followed her out of the bedroom and down the hall to the living room. She ignored my comments, but I could still see the blush on her cheeks as she sat on the couch. I felt like a dick for walking in on her, but I honestly had no idea she would be doing that while I was gone. It never even crossed my mind as something to consider might happen.

I grabbed the take-out bags, got her food ready, then set up a TV tray for her so she could eat on the couch. I knew she was due for another pain pill, so I grabbed one and set it next to the glass of water I had brought for her as well.

"Thank you for dinner," she said softly, looking at the TV instead of me.

"You're welcome. Sorry about what just happened."

"I should have closed and locked the door. I didn't think you'd be that quick." She laughed softly but still refused to look at me.

"I thought it was a good idea to call the order in before I left so I wouldn't be gone too long. I was worried about leaving you on your own for too long."

Lia's stomach growled loudly, making her cheeks flush with color again. Her blushing was starting to become one of my favorite things to see.

"Well, I guess my stomach says it was a good move. Apparently, I'm hungrier than I thought." She smiled and picked up the remote, looking for something to watch so we didn't have to talk to each other.

I cleaned up and put the leftovers in the fridge while Lia laid down on the couch. I knew she was getting tired, and it was already late, but I didn't want her sleeping there, no matter how comfortable she insisted it was.

"Do you want me to help you to bed?" I offered, wiping my hands on a towel before tossing it to the counter behind me. I loved that the kitchen and living room were technically all one room, which made it easy to keep an eye on her.

"I might just sleep here," she said sleepily, sinking lower into the cushions.

"While I appreciate how comfortable it is, I think you would do better in bed. Here, give me your hands, and I'll help you up."

I stood next to the couch and extended my hands to her, surprised when she actually accepted them. I moved slowly, giving her room to step with her good foot while getting her balance before putting her casted foot down. She swayed slightly, my instincts quickly forcing me to wrap my arms around her waist to steady her. I held her body tightly against mine, noticing the way her eyes changed the second she felt my touch.

There was electricity running through us, every little touch a new spark that threatened to ignite a flame. I pulled away slowly, making sure she was steady while I tried to ignore the way my body was responding to hers.

Fifteen
Lia

I ignored the way my body felt when Mason touched me. I had already had an eventful *and embarrassing* enough day as it was; I didn't need to entertain the thought that he might be interested in me ONLY to have him turn around and reject me. Because I knew at the end of the day, that would be what happened. He would be the mature, level-headed adult he always was and would give me a list of reasons why we couldn't act on the chemistry that was so obviously there between us—even if I *hated* to admit it.

I made it to the bathroom and closed the door behind me while I got ready for bed. I balanced the best I could at the sink while I washed my face, flossed, and brushed my teeth. It was a bit hard being on my foot for so long without being able to redistribute my weight, but I had skipped everything last night, so there was no way in hell I was going to skip tonight. I was thankful for the quick shower this morning, even if it was a pain in the ass to get done.

Once I finished, I pulled open the door and wiggled around it, making sure not to drop the crutches or bang my foot against anything as I made my way across the hall to my bedroom. Mason was already changed into a pair of low-hung sweatpants and no fucking shirt. He was just sitting on *my bed* with his stupid rock-solid abs that glistened perfectly in the light as he stared at something on his phone.

I rolled my eyes, frustrated with myself for being so attracted to the enemy, and made my way over to where I planned to sleep. It was my bed—okay, technically, it was Jones's bed, but that was beside the point. If Mason insisted on staying here tonight, he would have to figure something else out. Sharing a bed with him again was officially off the table after I slept like shit last night.

I pushed past him, making it apparent how much he was in my way when I smacked him in the back of the head with a pillow as I fluffed it. He reached back and grabbed it, never taking his eyes off his phone to acknowledge me. It was like he had stealthy cat reflexes and knew my next move before I even made it. I grabbed the other pillow and went to strike again, but this time, he grabbed my wrist and held it tightly in his grip as he continued reading whatever was on his phone. I leaned around his head, not caring that I was being rude by looking at what was on the screen. Whatever was holding his attention so strongly now had mine.

A loud gasp escaped as I leaned closer, my breasts brushing against his back as he maintained his hold on my wrist as I stared at the image of a pink bullet vibrator—much like the one I'd thrown at his head earlier.

"What are you doing?" I hissed, reaching for his phone with my free hand while trying to keep myself upright. I had my bad leg lifted onto the bed and rested my knee so I didn't accidentally step down and put weight on my injured ankle. "Why are you looking that up?"

"I had questions," he answered matter-of-factly, pulling his phone out of my grasp. "And since you wouldn't answer them, I was looking them up myself."

My eyebrows shot up on my forehead as I continued to reach for it. Just then, I lost my balance and started to fall when *stealthy cat Mason* turned and wrapped his arms around me, pulling me against his body in a tight embrace. We looked like one of those super romantic couples you see on TV where the guy dips the girl and then leans in to kiss her… but that wasn't us.

The air rushed out of my lungs as I felt his hard body against mine. His strong arms held me against his chest, the same one that was now rising and falling heavily as his eyes quickly searched mine, looking for something. Instinctively, I wet my lips, needing moisture as my throat felt dry and my heart raced wildly.

"Are you okay?" he asked, still not loosening his hold on me. His voice was deeper than usual, sending a chill that snaked up my spine and sent a shiver through me.

I nodded, too afraid to speak. All of my brain cells were currently being used to dissect what these stupid feelings I was feeling were as the butterflies swarmed in my stomach and my temperature rose a few degrees.

He set his phone down on the bed, still not taking his hands off me. Instead, he adjusted the one on my back, lowering it dangerously close to my ass. I inhaled sharply, not sure whether the aching in between my thighs was because I hadn't been touched in so long or if it was because *Mason* was touching me.

I shook my head, desperate to clear the fog. This was not something I saw coming, and now that he was holding me like a prized possession, I couldn't ignore the thoughts racing through my head.

Mason's fingers gently brushed against my back, allowing me to get lost in the warmth of his embrace, when suddenly my phone started ringing. A few seconds passed before I snapped out of it and attempted to get up in search of it.

"Here, let me help you," he offered, lifting me up and then setting me on the bed as if I weighed nothing. He grabbed my phone and handed it to me, then turned and left the room to give me some privacy.

"Hey," I answered. "How are things in California? Have you and my brother killed each other yet?" I was already rambling, which was a good indication of how frazzled I felt.

Kensy laughed softly as I heard my brother talking to someone in the background.

"You know, before this trip, I would have said that there was no way I would ever consider it, but seeing how long he takes to finish a sample of wine is quickly changing my mind about that," she said and then hiccupped.

"It's a *wine tasting*, Kensy. Not a girl's night with my sister," my brother said loud enough for me to hear.

"Tell him to stop being such a girl." I shifted on the bed, frustrated with how flat the pillow was behind me. It had only been one night, but that was enough for me to fall in love with the pillows Mason had.

"That's what I told him earlier! He's taken the sampling to the next level by sniffing it and swirling it around in the glass before taking the *teeniest, tiniest* sip."

"Is he lifting his pinky when he does?" I asked, imagining the look on his face as he listened to us make fun of him.

"YES!! He DOES!" she squealed and then screamed as his voice got closer.

"Stop telling lies, Kensy, or I'm going to make you pay for it later," he warned.

"Eeew. Gross. If you guys are going to start that shit, I'm hanging up."

"We're not," Kensy assured me. "I was calling to check in to see how you were doing."

"I'm fine. Managing the best I can and trying to get used to the crutches."

"I still feel bad that we're not there. We only have a few days left here, and then we can head home instead of stopping in Las Vegas."

"No. I'm fine. Don't cut your trip short for me."

"I can't go to Vegas and have fun knowing that you're stuck at home with a broken ankle."

"Sure you can. Just imagine I'm there throwing back shots like a champ instead of my sissy pinky-lifting wuss of a brother."

"I heard that."

"Good, maybe you'll stop drinking your wine like a pretentious little bitch," I teased, chewing my nail as I waited for his sarcastic comeback. We've always been close, but that didn't mean we didn't harass each other every single chance we got.

"So, how are things with Doctor Hottie?" Kensy asked, changing the subject.

"Things with Dr. Dickhead are fine," I replied right as he walked back into the room and arched an eyebrow. Apparently, the guys were hearing everything tonight. I shifted uncomfortably on the bed, knowing he was still listening.

"I'm sure it's hard getting used to crutches on top of being in a new place again. You just got used to Jones's place, now to have to get used to his."

"I'm actually back at Jones's," I said quietly, watching as Mason dug through his duffle bag.

"You are?"

"Yeah."

"Okay, there's definitely more to the story. Spill it."

I took a deep breath and slowly let it out as Mason walked out and shut the door behind him.

"I tried running away from him yesterday," I blurted out.

"You what?"

"I didn't want to be there anymore, so I got on my crutches and made a run for it."

"What happened?"

"I didn't get far. He finished in the shower and caught me as I was almost to the door."

"Why didn't you just tell him you wanted to leave?"

"I did. He keeps fighting me on it. I told him I wanted to come get some stuff, so he came with me. I asked him to check the mail, and when he did, I locked him out of the house, forgetting that he had the keys. I locked the deadbolt and chain lock up front, but he got in through the back door. It's like he's this constant shadow, always following me around. He's convinced that I can't take care of myself, so he's made sure he's always on top of me."

"Oh my!" Kensy giggled, completely taking that the wrong way.

"Not like that," I scolded playfully. "You have to get your mind out of the gutter."

"I can't. You're literally living the life of the girls in the steamy romance books I read. The poor heroine breaks her leg and has to be saved by the handsome doctor who wants to give her all the hands-on care she can take—"

"He better not be putting his hands on my fucking sister," my brother warned loudly.

"Oh, calm down," Kensy shot back at him. "It's not like your sister couldn't use a stress reliever or two right now."

"Kensy!" I shrieked at the same time my brother said something in the background.

"What? We all know it's true. Bella told me she hooked you up with some toys before they left."

"Yeah, she hooked me up, alright," I muttered quietly, my cheeks flaming hot when I remembered what happened earlier. "I'm starting to get drowsy from the pain meds. Mind if I call you tomorrow?"

"Not at all. Get some rest, and I'll text you to see how things are going. If you need anything, call me. I'm constantly checking flights back and can have something booked within minutes."

"Okay. Goodnight, Kens." I hung up the phone and tossed it on the bed, resting my head against the headboard for a few minutes before I had to deal with Mason again.

<u>Sixteen</u>

Mason

"Are you comfortable?" I frowned when I saw how flat the pillows were under Lia's leg, knowing that it wouldn't be enough to keep it elevated above her heart.

"I don't know what comfortable is anymore," she muttered, shifting again. "I hate these pillows."

"Yeah, I can see why. They look big and fluffy but go flat right away."

She pulled the one out from beneath her head and tossed it across the room in frustration.

"Where do you buy yours?"

"My pillows?" I turned and looked at her as I grabbed the extra pillows from my side of the bed.

She nodded, waiting for an answer.

"I order them online. Why?"

She laid her head flat and closed her eyes. I could tell that she was exhausted, and I wanted to get her as comfortable as possible so she could rest, but it was impossible with the current selection of pillows.

"I love your pillows."

I pulled my shoulders back and sat taller as an idea hit me.

"I'll be right back."

I climbed off the bed, making sure not to bump her leg, then rushed to the kitchen and grabbed the keys. I didn't know why I didn't think of it sooner, but my house was right next door, and I had the key to her comfort.

Knowing that Lia wasn't going to try to run away again now that she was where she wanted to be, I grabbed armfuls of pillows from my bed and then rushed back to find her already asleep on the bed. My shoulders slumped, knowing that I would end up waking her up as I got her leg situated, but at least now I had pillows.

I locked the doors and turned off most of the lights in the living room and kitchen. There were a few that had dimmers, so I set them to low in case Lia got up for any reason tonight and I didn't hear her. The last thing I wanted was for her to be trying to navigate through the house in the dark and trip and fall.

I was quiet when I went back into the room, making every effort not to wake her. I set the pillows on the floor and then gently lifted her leg as I piled two of them beneath it. Satisfied that it was elevated high enough, I grabbed another pillow and placed it under her head, ignoring the way her face immediately turned and cuddled into the palm of my hand.

We hadn't talked about the sleeping arrangement for tonight, but I was tired and didn't feel like trying to bring the air mattress over. I pulled a t-shirt over my head and then climbed into bed beside her, hating how it felt so right.

I laid down and pulled the other pillow under my head, thankful that the bed was relatively comfortable. I was so used to my bed that sleeping anywhere else was sure to leave me feeling sore the next day, but if Lia were comfier here, then I would figure out a way to make it work.

Her body was relaxed beside mine without any pillow barriers in between to separate us. The sound of her snoring quickly filled the room, followed by a fart. I grinned, knowing how mortified she would be to know that she was, in fact, the noisiest, stinkiest little mouse that ever slept and not the quiet one she imagined herself to be.

Fifth Wheel

<u>Seventeen</u>
Lia

A few days passed without Mason or I talking about what happened the other night in bed when he was practically holding me in his lap. I didn't want to bring it up and make him uncomfortable because, for all I knew, he didn't feel the same way as I had been feeling since it happened. Which was enraging, given how much I started out hating the guy. One quick touch of his body against mine and I was quickly melting into a puddle. How does that even happen??

Okay, so I knew how it happened. He had been wearing me down a little bit each day with his constant worrying about me and taking care of me. It would have been so much easier if he would have just let me be to fend for myself but *nooo*, he had to come in and rescue me even though I was convinced I didn't need saving.

It had been almost a week since I'd broken my ankle and I felt like a pro on crutches now. Our sleeping arrangement had been decided the first night he slept here—without my input because I was already asleep. And even though I would *never* admit it, I slept better when he was next to me. I mean, I slept even better in his stupid bed with the pillow top mattress and fluffy pillows, but I was never going to admit that. Just like I wasn't going to admit that I was starting to worry about how deeply I was attracted to him.

He was currently at the grocery store, picking up stuff for the week after I gave him a short list of what I needed. He had been doing all of the cooking, and I was irritated by how much better his eggplant parmigiana was than mine. Hell, everything he cooked was better than anything I made. I had expected to give in and break my healthy eating streak while everyone was out of town, but then Mason stepped in and made it easy to stay on top of it. Between protein shakes and real salads, we hardly ate out, and it was weird that I no longer had a craving for Tipsy Taquito like I usually would. I had a craving for something else, but *that* wasn't on the menu.

I felt restless as I hopped around the house, looking for something to do. In addition to cooking for me, he had also taken care of the cleaning. I was still convinced that he was from some romance novel, too good to be true. I mean, I grew up with a brother who was 99% pure caveman until Kensy moved in with him, and then suddenly, he was a changed man.

The sun was shining, and I desperately wanted to go outside and soak it up for a little bit but I knew that Mason would be mad that I didn't wait for him to help me. But the truth was that he only had another week off of work, so I had no choice but to start figuring things out on my own anyway. Kensy and my brother would be back this weekend, but Bella and Jones were taking a little detour and wouldn't be back for another week or two, which meant I would still be on my own for a while longer. There was NO WAY in hell I would go stay with my brother and be stuck having to watch them make out like horny teenagers. No thanks.

I hobbled to my bedroom, fished my bikini out of the drawer, and got changed. I debated on taking a toy outside with me, given the built-up tension that was constantly lingering between my legs, but after the last time, I wasn't about to risk it. It would be just my luck that he would walk in on me again. I would have to find some other way to take care of it during one of the few times he left me alone in the house.

I adjusted the straps of the pink polka-dot bikini top and turned to admire how good my butt looked in the high-cut bottoms. Since I couldn't go to the beach, the least I could do was get some much-needed vitamin D here. I grabbed my phone, ChapStick, and a bottle of sunscreen and shoved them into a tote bag so I wouldn't have to try to carry everything. Then I went to the kitchen, grabbed a few snacks and a couple of drinks, adding them to the bag. It was heavy and kind of hard to balance on my shoulder without knocking it off with my crutch, but I managed. There was no way I was going to go back and forth later to get the things I needed. It was better just to do it all now.

Once I opened the back door, I stopped and closed my eyes, allowing the warmth from the sun to kiss my body. The backyard wasn't big, but it wasn't too small either. Jones had an area set up for the grill, a patio table with soft, padded chairs, and a few chaise lounge chairs that were calling my name. I balanced the best I could as I slipped the crutch out from beneath my arm, grabbed the tote bag, and set it in the chair beside me. I almost lost my balance and squinted my eyes closed as I tried to steady myself, thankful when I didn't fall.

I took a deep breath in and slowly exhaled as I took my time sitting down and resting my crutches on the chair beside me. I had forgotten to grab my sunglasses, but that didn't matter right now. I was outside, enjoying some alone time in the sun without a care in the world. I leaned back, closed my eyes, and let myself relax for the first time in a long time.

I had no idea how long I had been asleep, but Mason's deep voice startled me out of it. I blinked quickly, trying to focus as the heavy fog started to lift.

"What are you doing out here, Lia?" he asked, standing above me as he blocked the sun. A sudden chill ran through me, but I wasn't sure if it was from the lack of warmth from the sun or the sight of Mason in front of me.

"I wanted to come outside and get some fresh air," I answered, suddenly feeling very on display as he made no effort to keep his eyes from roaming over my body in my tiny bikini. Even though I deliberately put it on to see his reaction to it, I hadn't expected to feel so vulnerable about it.

"You're turning red. Did you put sunscreen on?"

"No, *Dad*," I answered, already getting annoyed with his condescending tone. It was funny how quickly that happened with him. "I meant to, but I closed my eyes for a second and must have fallen asleep."

He shook his head and closed his eyes.

"You know skin cancer is a real thing, right?"

I arched an eyebrow at him, eyes narrowed as I refused to answer.

"I'm just saying you need to be more careful, Lia. I get wanting to be outside and enjoy the warm—or rather *hot* weather, but you need to be smart about it."

"Hey, I am smart about it," I countered with a hint of anger in my tone. "I brought sunscreen. I just *accidentally* fell asleep before I could put it on. It's not like I purposely refused to put it on."

"Do you want me to help you, or are you heading in?"

"No, I'm not heading in. I was going to figure out a way to turn over so I can tan my back."

It was his turn to arch an eyebrow at me as he folded his arms over his chest.

"I don't think that's the best idea."

"And why not?"

"I hate to be the bearer of bad news, but it's probably going to be hard—if not impossible—to roll over onto your stomach and not hurt yourself. You have a broken ankle that's in a cast."

"Do you think I've somehow forgotten about this pain in the ass cast? Trust me, if anyone is aware of it—it's me. You don't have to help me, but you sure as hell don't get to stand here and scold me like I'm some kid."

"I'm sorry. I wasn't trying to upset you. I simply worry about you being out here by yourself, asleep in the sun."

My shoulders relaxed slightly, surprised by his apology.

"So, do you want me to help you?"

"It depends. What are you going to help with?"

"Whatever you need."

"Like turning over so I can tan my back?" I asked, knowing I was pressing my luck. I knew it would be difficult, and the chances of hurting my foot in the process were high if I did it on my own, but if he helped, we might have better luck.

"Fine," he said with a heavy sigh. "Let me lower the back of the chair for you real quick."

I leaned forward and ignored the way his cologne floated in the air around me as he moved. I wanted to get a nice tan for the summer, but I also didn't want tan lines. While his back was turned to me, I took the opportunity to untie the top in the back, clutching the front to my chest.

"Alright, if you want to start turning face down, I'll grab your leg and help guide you."

I nodded, wondering if I should just forget about the bikini top since I needed my hands for this. I tossed it to the side, hearing a low growl behind me as I grabbed hold of the sides of the chair and lowered myself onto it. Mason gently held my leg until I was situated and then laid it down.

"Where is the sunscreen?" he asked.

I turned my head and pointed to the tote bag on the chair beside me.

"It's in there."

He reached for the bag but then stopped and looked at me.

"Am I going to find any *surprises* in here?"

"No. You're fine, you big baby."

"Hey, you're not the one who got hit in the head with it. It's surprising how much it hurt, given how little it was."

He opened the bag and started digging through it as I laid my head down and closed my eyes. It felt so good out here with the sun warming my skin that nothing else could compare. Mason's hands were soft against my skin as he rubbed the lotion over my back, gently massaging as he worked it into my skin. Okay—I was wrong. Mason touching my body was far better than anything the sun could do.

Eighteen

Mason

Rubbing sunscreen onto Lia's body—knowing she was topless right now—was enough to give me a raging boner instantly. I tried to keep my distance as I worked the lotion into her skin, but there were parts I couldn't reach without getting closer.

I sat down on the edge beside her, careful not to focus on the side boob that was less than an inch away from my leg. I squirted more lotion onto my hand and continued rubbing it along her lower back, groaning inside with how low her bikini bottoms rode. If she moved even a fraction of an inch, I would see butt crack. I shifted myself again, frustrated with my body for acting like a horny teenager as I rushed to try to get this over with.

"Thank you for helping with this," she said softly, moving her hair out of the way as I made my way up her back and began rubbing it across the tops of her shoulders and neck. My fingers did what they wanted instead of what I was telling them to do, massaging the muscles that had to be tense and sore from the crutches. She whimpered softly, arching her back to lean into my touch as I continued to massage her.

"That feels sooo good," she whispered, and my dick hardened even more. "I'll give you whatever you want if you don't stop."

"I won't stop, baby. I want to make you feel good." The words slipped out, rolling effortlessly off my tongue before I could stop them.

"Here, maybe this will help." She lifted on her elbows, pushing her back closer to me. But in doing so, it also gave me a glimpse of her breasts hanging heavily, begging for me to reach forward and cradle them in my hands.

I continued massaging her the best I could, but I felt like I was going to explode any second. I didn't want to cross the line with Lia and if we kept going the way we were, it was bound to happen. I rushed through the rest of it, making sure her back and arms were entirely covered with sunscreen before slamming the bottle down beside her.

"I need to go inside and put the groceries away," I said randomly, turning to leave before she could question what happened.

I went inside and left the door open so I could hear if she needed anything. There were groceries that needed to be put away, but I had a growing problem that needed to be handled immediately. I stalked down the hallway, grabbed the bottle of lotion I had seen Lia use last night, and then locked myself in the bathroom.

With frustration and arousal raging through me, I unzipped my pants, pulled my cock out, and began stroking it. I was hard as a rock and needed relief right away. I squirted some lotion into the palm of my hand and jerked it as I pictured Lia outside.

I imagined how good it would have felt to turn her over and suck her nipples, tugging hard at them until I brought her to climax while fingering her wet pussy and rubbing her clit. I had no idea what she liked or what would get her off, but I knew I could do more to please her than that stupid small bullet she was using the other day. I hadn't been able to stop thinking about it—let alone comparing myself to it—since then.

My cock didn't vibrate, but it could still rub her clit the right way and fuck her senseless. I pictured her taking it in her mouth, her eyes watering as she gagged on my length while taking me into the back of her throat. I gripped myself harder, jerking faster as I closed my eyes and saw her riding me, her head thrown back in ecstasy as she used my cock for her own pleasure until she came.

I bit the inside of my lip, my teeth digging into it so hard the pain was almost unbearable as I reached for a tissue and shot ropes of cum into it. It wasn't the relief I really wanted, but it would have to do since Lia was still off-limits.

Once I cleaned up, I went to the kitchen and put the groceries away after making sure she was okay. She was still lying on her stomach, but I couldn't tell whether she had fallen asleep again. From what I could see through the window, she wasn't burning, so I let her be while I figured out what to make for dinner.

I knew that Lia had been enjoying the healthy meals I had been making, but I also knew how much she loved her fried food from Tipsy Taquito. She had mentioned that she was trying to eat better, and I didn't want to sabotage her by picking up food from there tonight, so I grabbed the stuff to make tacos at home. It was already after five, but I didn't know what time she wanted to eat, so I worked on making margaritas and putting them in the fridge to chill until we were ready. Soon, I didn't have anything else to prep for dinner, so I went outside to check on Lia.

"Are you fully cooked now?" I asked, leaning against the wall to refrain from touching her.

She lifted her head and smiled up at me before attempting to roll over onto her back. I grabbed her bikini top from the ground and tossed it to her before looking away.

"Thanks."

I nodded but kept staring at the wall, hating the way my cock was already hardening again knowing that her tits were begging for me to look at them.

"What time did you want to eat tonight?" I asked, feeling like an idiot for talking to the wall.

"We can eat whenever. I just need a shower to cool me off, and then my appetite will be back."

I could hear her moving around and debating on checking to see if she needed help so she didn't hurt her leg.

"I'm fully clothed now. You don't have to keep staring at the wall, Doc."

I turned and gave her a look that said I begged to differ as my eyes pointedly traveled the length of her body. Her cheeks flushed red as she tucked a strand of hair behind her ear.

"Did you want to take a shower now?" I asked, hating that my cock was reacting to thoughts of her naked and wet as I helped her.

"If you don't mind, that would be great. Then I can help you with dinner."

I walked over and extended my arms to help her up, gently lifting and pulling her against my body as she stood up. She smelled like coconut and sunshine, a combination I could easily get used to. I reached down and grabbed her crutches, helping her on them before guiding her inside and to the shower. At this rate, I was going to need an ice-cold one to chill myself the fuck out.

<u>Nineteen</u>
Lia

I was on my second margarita as I tried to keep from spitting a mouthful of taco at Mason as another laugh erupted out of me. I had no idea what he put in the drinks, but they made me feel lighter than a feather, and everything he said was funny. *Had Mason always been funny and I was just too busy hating him to notice?*

"You're kidding!" I squealed, shifting on the couch to see him better. He wiped at his mouth with a napkin, shaking his head as his grin spread wider.

"I swear to God, she took out her dentures and offered me a blow job if I would take the IV out and release her."

"How old was she?"

"Late eighties. She didn't want to be there, and I got it, but still, it was not my cup of tea." He scrunched his face, his whole body shaking.

"You know, I feel like med school really hasn't prepared me for the real world," I joked, taking another sip.

"Na, you'll be fine. What specialty did you decide on?"

"So far, pediatrics. I'm supposed to start my summer job in a few weeks once Jane is back from vacation."

I frequented Rockin' Rooster for my pastry and coffee fix so often that I had gotten to know the owner, Abby, very well over the past few years. When she told me that her sister would be needing help over the summer, it was a dream come true to be able to work in a pediatric office and getting some hands-on experience.

"I think that'll be a good fit for you," he replied with a warm smile. "But you'll have to be nice to the kids."

I lifted my glass to my lips but stopped, my eyes widening as I processed his words.

"What? I'm always nice!"

"Ugh, yeah, right." He started laughing as he lifted his taco and took a bite.

"Well, maybe not to you, but to other people."

"Why are you so mean to me anyway?" He wiped his mouth again, his tongue slipping out just enough to lick a crumb from his lip, leaving a shimmery wetness behind.

I pressed my legs closed and tried to remember what he asked me instead of thinking about how good his tongue would feel on my clit.

"I don't know," I admitted with a shrug. "I guess you just rubbed me the wrong way."

His eyes lit up at my words as a devilish smile spread across his face again.

"I can guarantee you that I would never *rub you* the wrong way, Lia."

A chill shot up my spine as a burst of heat flushed through me. I set my glass down on the table and stared down at my plate of food, unsure of how to answer that. Did he mean for the sexual innuendo to come through, or was I just hearing things the way I wanted to hear them?

"What's wrong? Cat got your tongue?"

I looked up at him, noticing something different in his features. His shoulders were down, and his body looked more relaxed overall. Even his fingers as he gripped the taco in between them before lifting it to his mouth and taking the sexiest bite I'd ever seen.

"No, but it's about to have yours if you don't stop," I mumbled quietly under my breath before trying to distract myself with eating.

I couldn't tell if we were actually flirting with each other or if we'd just had enough tequila to lower the walls we'd put up. Okay, that *I'd* put up. But still, this was kinda nice, even if I didn't want to admit it.

I took a bite and was chewing when Mason lowered his taco to his plate and looked at me.

"Why do you like tiny dick?"

My eyes widened as I swallowed, the food in my mouth not yet small enough to get down right before I started choking. I reached for my glass and took a drink, hoping to wash it down before he had to give me the Heimlich maneuver. The last thing I needed was for Mason to have to save me again.

I coughed hard, taking a few more sips until I was sure the food had made its way down before trying to answer.

"What?" I asked, still in shock.

"The teeny tiny vibrator thing," he clarified as if this was normal, everyday conversation. "Why do you like it so much? Have you only been with guys who have micro penises?"

I shook my head, hoping that would shake the answer loose, but it didn't.

"I honestly don't know where you came up with that idea from, but no, I don't like micro penises."

"Then why such a small vibrator?" His brows pinched together in confusion.

"I guess because it's supposed to be a travel one?" I shrugged. "I honestly don't know. My friend got it for me from the company she works with."

"Isn't it kind of hard to… you know… use?"

I rubbed my lips together, trying to form the right answer to that question. Typically, I would die having this kind of conversation with a man, but this felt different. Maybe it was the margaritas—okay—it was *definitely* the margaritas, but it also felt different in general with Mason.

"I don't stick it inside myself or anything," I finally said after what felt like forever. He was still staring at me, giving me the look he used when he was trying to diagnose a patient in the ER.

"I don't get it."

"It's for clitoral stimulation," I replied with a laugh. "It's not like a full-size dildo you fuck yourself with. It's just for girls to help get the job done."

"Why not have your partner do that?"

"Well, first of all, I don't have a partner. Second, every single guy that I've been with hasn't been able to get me off, so I'm thinking that it's not as common as you think it is, Doc."

He furrowed his brow deeper and leaned into the cushion behind him.

"None of them?"

"None. Zero. Zip. Zelch. Nada."

"Wow. Well, I guess that explains a lot about the toy then."

I nodded, feeling slightly embarrassed that I'd just admitted that to him.

"But you have one with the… you know… toy?" he asked, shifting as if he were uncomfortable.

"Usually. When people don't barge in and scare the crap out of me," I teased.

"Sorry about that. I hate that you didn't get the relief you were looking for more than I hate to admit that I got hit in the forehead with a tiny dick."

"Technically, it's not a dick," I corrected. "It's a bullet."

"I guess that makes me sound more manly."

"I mean, I wouldn't go around bragging about it." I giggled and set my plate down on the coffee table.

"True." He nodded in agreement. "Thanks for finally telling me why you like it. Google wasn't helpful at all, and I stumbled upon some stuff I can't ever unsee."

"I can only imagine the stuff you found."

"It's worse than anything I've seen in the ER."

"Okay, now that's scary!"

My body relaxed against the couch as we laughed and talked. Surprisingly, I had a good time with the guy I thought I hated.

<u>Twenty</u>

Mason

"You ready for bed?" I asked as I loaded the margarita glasses into the dishwasher and started it.

Lia yawned and sank lower into the couch, clearly relaxed and tired.

"I'm so comfortable here," she whined. "Don't make me get up and go in there."

"How else am I supposed to keep an eye on you if you're not in the bed with me?"

"I don't know. Sooner or later, you're going back to work, so you won't be able to keep watching me like a hawk. We can start now. A trial run." Her eyes fluttered closed as she rested her head against the pillow.

My jaw tightened at the thought of having to return to work and not being here to take care of her. I knew that her friends were supposed to be back soon, but I didn't like the idea of leaving her by herself, even with them being there to help her.

"Maybe I like watching you. Have you ever stopped to think about that?"

The margaritas must have still been flowing through my veins because my words were coming of their own free will, and I didn't feel inclined to try to stop them.

"Like when you walked in on me the other day? Were you trying to catch a show then, Doc?"

"No, I honestly had no idea you would be doing that." I sat on the arm of the chair next to her and looked down at her. She looked beautiful lying there, so peaceful. "But you bet your ass I would have stayed and watched if you invited me."

Her eyes flew open, locking onto mine. But I didn't flinch or look away. I held her gaze and let her see the desire pooling in mine that I had been trying so hard to fight.

"You would watch me?" she asked, her voice nearly a whisper.

"I would do whatever you allowed me to, Lia. I would watch you get yourself off with a tiny vibrating dick if that's all you gave me. I would take you to bed and show you how easy it is to bring you to climax without the help of a toy. I would fuck you so good that you wouldn't be able to walk right for days, and it would have nothing to do with your broken ankle."

"It's a bullet," she corrected with a cheeky grin.

"Out of all of that I just said, *that's* what you're focusing on?"

She shrugged and tried to keep from smiling more.

"I mean, you have to get the facts right."

"Fine, I'll gladly watch you get yourself off with a *bullet*."

"What about the other stuff?"

"I would do that too."

"Okay, so what are you waiting for?"

I pulled in a deep breath, my conscience talking louder than my cock.

"Another time," I said as lightly as I could.

"Wait—you're going to sit there and say all that to me but then not act on any of it?"

"Not when we've both been drinking. If anything happens between us, I want to know that we are both clear-headed and aware of the decisions we make. Mutual consent is a must for me, Lia. I won't do anything if I feel there's even the slightest doubt that you might not want it to happen."

"I am literally giving you my consent right now. Do you want me to sign something? Lift my hand and solemnly swear? What do you need from me besides the words that are coming from my mouth?"

"You're cute when you get fired up, but the answer is no. Not tonight."

She narrowed her eyes at me and squared her shoulders.

"I see you're back to being Dr. Dickhead."

I knew she was pissed, and rightfully so. I shouldn't have allowed myself to say the things I said to her, even if I was a little more relaxed from the drinks. But I couldn't in good conscience do anything intimate with her, not knowing whether she would make the same decision without having alcohol in her system. I was raised better than that and held my head high, knowing that I would die on the hill of mutual consent and respect being a staple in every relationship.

"I'm just trying to do the right thing, Lia."

"Well, it seems like if that was true, I would be screaming your name as an orgasm ripped through me before being fucked senseless, as you claim. But hey, I get it. Sometimes, the pressure to perform can be too much, and I wouldn't want you to be embarrassed if you couldn't deliver."

I worked my jaw back and forth in frustration, refusing to engage in this conversation with her any longer. Instead, I bent down and grabbed her crutches before offering them to her. She yanked them out of my hands and glared at me, her blue eyes icier than a glacier.

"Here, let me help you," I offered, trying to assist with getting the crutches lined up right.

"I've got it," she snapped. "Trust me, I can *take care* of myself."

She didn't look at me as she walked past and stormed down the hall to the bedroom. The door slammed shut a few seconds later, making it clear that I would not be sleeping in there with her tonight.

I exhaled heavily, tilting my head back and closing my eyes as I scolded myself for allowing this to happen in the first place. I'd fucked up by talking to her like that and then not acting on my words, but one day, she would appreciate the restraint it took to not burst into her room and fuck that attitude out of her.

<u>Twenty-One</u>
Lia

I was being a total bitch, and I knew it.

But it wasn't my fault.

Okay, so it was partly my fault. I had been drinking and flirting with Mason all night, encouraging him to talk to me the way he did. Which, by the way, I didn't mind one bit. What I did mind was that he suddenly changed his mind about everything and essentially turned me down when I was already getting hot and bothered by his dirty words. And I couldn't stop imagining what else he might say if we gave in to this stupid lust that kept sizzling between us every chance it got.

It would be better if I went back to hating Dr. Dickhead. Then that way, neither of us would have to worry about being embarrassed if we ran into each other at the hospital since nothing would have happened. But the problem was that I didn't want us to go back to how we were before. Now that I'd gotten to know Mason while being cooped up in the same house with him for a week, it was getting a lot harder to hate him.

As much as I despised admitting it, he was actually a really nice guy. He always put my needs above his, checking to make sure I had everything I needed and that I was comfortable. He took it upon himself to manage my pain meds while caring for my broken ankle, even when he didn't have to. I didn't ask him for a single thing, yet he kept giving so selflessly.

I lay in bed wondering what would have happened if he hadn't said no. Would we be cuddled up together, coming down from mind-blowing sex? Or would he be between my legs, showing me how well he could work his tongue to bring me to ecstasy? It wasn't like I had anything to use as a point of reference for how good Mason was in bed, but something told me I was definitely missing out.

The next morning, I woke up disappointed to find the other side of the bed empty. Even though I was being a bitch to Mason and slammed the door shut, part of me had hoped that he would be the determined bastard he'd been in the very beginning and force his way in to check on me.

But maybe this was how things were supposed to be. It'd been over a week since I'd broken my ankle, so I'd had plenty of time to get used to the crutches and learn how to wrap it myself so I could shower. Having Mason take care of me was quickly turning into a luxury, not a necessity.

I yawned, still tired after a restless night of very little sleep, and got out of bed. I hated how easy it was to maneuver on my own, which was funny given how desperately I wanted this from the very start—back when I truly hated Mason.

The smell of coffee brewing filled the air as I made my way to the bathroom. I needed to pee, but I also needed some Tylenol for the pounding headache that greeted me first thing when I opened my eyes. Last night had been fun, but maybe next time, we should take it easy on the margaritas. *If* there was a next time.

I opened the medicine cabinet and grabbed a few pills before popping them in my mouth. I leaned forward the best I could to cup my hand in the water from the sink, taking a drink without getting too much water everywhere. I wiped up the mess with a towel and took a look at myself in the mirror.

My hair was piled loosely on my head, looking like some sort of prehistoric bird's nest. I pulled the hair tie out and grabbed the brush, running it through quickly as I struggled to hold myself up on the crutches. There were dark circles under my eyes, and my skin looked pale. I couldn't honestly blame Mason for not wanting to be with me if this was what he saw.

I debated taking a full shower right now or coming back to do it later, but the last thing I wanted was for him to see me like this. I grabbed the stuff I needed and wrapped my cast while I waited for the water to heat up. I hadn't bothered to grab clean clothes since I wasn't planning on taking a shower right now, to begin with, but I would just have to improvise. I was going to start making an effort again, which meant I would figure out how to do my hair and makeup without hurting my foot.

By the time I was done, the water was going cold but that's what happens when you attempt to take an *everything* shower. I shaved the best I could, hoping I reached the most important parts before giving up. I shampooed and conditioned my hair while taking the time to use the new sugar scrub I bought before I broke my ankle. Not only did I smell good, but my body felt good. Hangover or not, I now had the confidence I needed to face Mason after what happened last night.

I balanced myself on one crutch, keeping my weight off of my foot, as I applied another coat of mascara to my lashes. I had wanted to go all out with getting ready, but it was already more painful than I imagined, so I did what I could and hoped for the best. If I could manage to get *both* eyes done, that would be a win today. There would be nothing scarier than a girl with half a face of makeup done and the other half looking like she got run over by a tequila truck.

 My hair was still wet and tossed into a high bun on top of my head, but at least my makeup looked nice. I finished putting my lipstick on, rubbed my lips together to make sure it was even, then put the tube in my makeup bag with the other stuff.

I was still wearing a towel wrapped around my body since I didn't have clean clothes with me. I tucked the loose end in under my armpit and then opened the door, allowing the steam to rush out ahead of me. I left my dirty clothes on the floor for now, as my main concern was making it back to the bedroom without a wardrobe malfunction. Thankfully, it was just across the hall, so I didn't have far to go.

"Hey, I made breakfast," Mason said, coming around the corner and startling me.

I shrieked and spun around, losing the grip on my crutches as he came rushing over and grabbed me right as my towel came undone from the crutch trying to rip it off. *Was my crutch seriously trying to act like a wingman right now?*

The fabric had already started to fall down my body, stopping at my waist by the time I was able to grab it. His arms wrapped tightly around my back, steadying me before I could hurt myself.

"Are you okay?" he asked, having the courtesy not to look down as goosebumps quickly spread over my skin from the cold air rushing down over me from the air conditioner.

"I'm fine," I whispered, hating how my body tingled from his touch. I reached down and tried to grab the towel to pull it up but couldn't get a good grip on it.

"Here, let me."

I held my breath as his fingers trailed lightly over my skin, gently pulling the towel back where it belonged as he covered my breasts and attempted to tuck the corner back in place.

"Thank you," I said, clearing my throat.

"No problem."

He was still standing right in front of me, not making any effort to move as my body screamed for him to touch me again.

"I should—"

Before I could say anything, Mason cupped the back of my head and lowered his mouth to mine. The warmth and softness of his lips made my body come to life as I leaned into his touch and wrapped my arms around the back of his neck.

It was the kiss I wanted last night, the kiss I hadn't stopped thinking about as I tried fingering myself to get off when I couldn't stop the aching between my thighs. The kiss that haunted my dreams as restless sleep reminded me of the yearning desire I still needed satisfied.

I moaned into it, his tongue darting out as it eagerly explored my mouth.

I wanted to lift my legs and wrap them around his waist, but it was impossible with the stupid cast on. Instead, I pressed myself even harder against him, gasping when I felt the hard outline of his erection. I pulled away and looked up at him, wanting to confirm he was as aroused by this as I was.

"Mason," I panted, gripping his short locks of hair in my fingers as he kissed down the side of my neck.

"Mmm hmmm."

"Get me a pen and paper," I moaned.

"What?" he asked with a laugh as he pulled away and looked at me.

"I'm putting my consent in writing because if you don't fuck me this time, I might literally die."

He chuckled and leaned in, planting more gentle kisses along my collarbone.

"Don't worry, I know CPR."

"Does it need to be mouth to mouth, or can it be—"

"Oh!" I yelped, unable to finish my sentence or think properly as he nipped my earlobe, sending a jolt right through me. One hand stayed wrapped firmly around my back while the other moved around and untucked the towel, letting it drop to the floor.

"I thought mouth to pussy might be needed," he said coyly, his lips brushing over my mouth again. "But I need to see how wet you are first. Why don't you be a good girl and lie down on the bed so I can do a proper exam?"

If someone had told me a month ago that I would be turned on by Dr. Dickhead talking dirty to me and almost role-playing the whole *doctor* thing—I would have told them they were out of their freaking minds. But this—oh, I was totally here for this.

I accepted his help over to the bed and eagerly climbed up, not caring that I was fully naked and on display before him. His eyes slowly roamed over my body, soaking in every tiny detail as he reached back and pulled his shirt over his head before tossing it to the floor.

"If at any time you want to stop, you have to tell me. Okay, Lia?"

I nodded and shuddered as his finger reached out and popped my lip free from being held between my teeth.

"No, I need to hear you say it. Tell me you'll say something if you want to stop whatever we're doing."

"I will say something if I want to stop. But right now, I need you to touch me, please," I begged. "Or get me my toy. Something. Anything." I squeezed my legs tightly together as if that would stop the ache between them.

I closed my eyes and squirmed on the bed, my body already overstimulated just by the thoughts of what he might do to me.

"Relax, Lia," he coaxed gently, lying beside me. "We're not rushing this so I'm going to need you to try to relax and enjoy me touching you. Okay?"

"I've been dying to come for days," I whined. "I can't relax. I'm all knotted up in this big ball of frustration. Really, if you give me a toy out of that drawer, I can get myself off real quick. I'll even let you watch. Then we can move to the fun part and take care of you." I knew how desperate I sounded begging, but I was desperate and knew what I needed right now.

"Open your legs for me," he instructed, ignoring my request for a toy.

"Mason, please. Let's just go with what I know works."

"Lia—trust me and open your legs."

I exhaled heavily and did as he asked, keeping my eyes closed as I felt his fingers feather over my thighs.

"You're so wet," he whispered as a finger parted my folds and slipped inside. My back arched as I tried to breathe steadily. "Your clit is swollen and ready for me, baby."

I nodded, unable to speak, even though I wanted to tell him to get the toy so we could get this part over with and move on. I didn't need him to take his time and admire my body; I just needed to climax.

His finger rubbed inside me as he pushed it in and out, building incredible friction that I wanted more of, but I couldn't think about anything other than coming.

"Look at how greedily she's gripping my fingers," he commented after adding another one. "Just imagine how well she's going to milk my cock in a few minutes."

"Please, Mason. The toy," I panted, taking quick, shallow breaths.

He shifted beside me, pulled his fingers out, then spread my wetness over my clit. I jerked hard, the feeling of his fingers on my most sensitive part almost too much to handle.

"Take deep breaths. Long, slow, deep breaths."

I did as he said and focused on my breathing as my body felt alive beneath his touch. I arched into it, pulling another deep breath in through my mouth and filling my lungs as he began rubbing my clit harder.

"Breathe, Lia."

I nodded and continued breathing as I felt myself on the edge of climax. I moaned and gripped the sheet beneath me as I tried to hold on as the first wave of pleasure washed over me. I immediately started panting and expected him to pull away, but he kept going.

"Deep breaths, baby."

I cried out as another jolt hit me, an orgasm more intense than I'd ever experienced before. I kept taking deep breaths, amazed by how he was able to draw every last bit of it out of me. By the time I was done, my body lay limp on the bed while he stared down at me with a satisfied smirk on his lips.

"That was incredible," I whispered, still trying to catch my breath.

"I told you you didn't need a toy."

"Nope. You're my new toy."

"I don't mind that one bit," he said, leaning over and kissing my forehead.

"I still want you to fuck me."

"I still want to fuck you."

"So, what are you waiting for?"

"You to catch your breath."

"You're quite obsessed with respiratory stuff. Are you sure you shouldn't have gone into pulmonary instead of the ER?"

"I want you to catch your breath because when I fuck you in a few minutes, I need to know you have enough oxygen to scream my name and let everyone know who's cock you're coming on."

Twenty-Two

Mason

Lia was beautiful, but she was even more gorgeous with sweat dotting her skin and a post-orgasm glow. I knew she would look even better with my cock deep inside her as I gave her body the full release she needed.

I knew that she wasn't going to allow herself to relax enough to enjoy anything until she came, so I made sure to get that out of the way right away. But now that she had, I couldn't stop thinking about how I wanted to see her face twisted in pleasure every day for the rest of my life. My cock twitched at the thought, desperate to explore her pussy that had wrapped so tightly around my fingers.

"We don't have too many options for different positions with your cast, but I can try to get creative if you want me to," I said softly as I leaned in and kissed my way across her shoulder before sliding down and pulling a pebbled nipple into my mouth.

"As long as your dick is inside of me, I don't care what position we're in. Hell, I'll stand on my head and go spread eagle if you need me to. Just fuck me, Mason."

I sucked harder, my hand dipping down between her thighs to find her soaking wet for me again.

"Let me run home and grab a condom real quick." I hated that I didn't have any with me, but it wasn't like I had temporarily moved over here with thoughts of fucking her on my mind.

"No, that'll take forever," she complained, grabbing my hand and jerking in and out of her as she fingered herself with my fingers. I grinned, loving how she was so freely using my body for her pleasure. "I'm on the pill and get tested regularly. I'm clean."

"Same."

Her eyes fluttered open as she gave me a quizzical look.

"I mean, I'm not on any pills other than a daily multivitamin. And I can't get pregnant, nor will I try to knock you up," I clarified, loving the little giggle that came out of her from my joke.

"Okay, let's do this."

"So impatient," I teased, slowly pulling my fingers out of her so I could take the rest of my clothes off.

"I'm a very needy girl—you knew this about me. Now hurry up and give me that cock."

"If you keep talking to me like that, I'm going to make you wait and punish you for being a brat."

I stood at the end of the bed, slowly pulling my joggers down, just to torment her as she waited with bated breath to see what I was packing.

"Oh yeah? Punish me how?" She lifted on her elbows and licked her lips. She was playing with fire, and I was more than happy to add some fuel to it.

"I'd start by putting my cock down your throat so you can't keep talking back. Then I'd spank that sweet little ass of yours, making sure my handprint stays so you know whose ass that is after I claim it."

"Such big talk for a man who's standing across the room with a raging boner that he has yet to set free," she said with a heavy sigh as if she were growing bored of this.

"I'm taking it slow because I don't want to scare you. It's quite large compared to those tiny dicks you've been fucking around with. Maybe I should contact that toy company your friend works at and see if they want a mold of the real thing. You know, increase user satisfaction and all that."

"No one is going to be satisfied if you keep standing there, talking."

"I don't know, I might be." I lowered my boxer briefs and grabbed my cock that was jutting up to my stomach as Lia's eyes widened. My hand gripped it tightly, slowly stroking the length as a drop of precum dotted the tip.

She licked her lips, her legs parting again as she watched.

"You make me so fucking hard," I gritted out between clenched teeth, desperately trying not to let myself get too worked up. I had been hard for Lia for days, and the constant jerking off in the shower wasn't doing anything to tame the beast right now.

"Show me," she whispered.

I continued stroking as I walked over and then climbed on the bed. I towered over her, which put my cock right at head level for her.

"Is this what you want?"

She nodded and swatted my hand away, replacing it with hers as she softly stroked me before licking the precum off the tip with her tongue. I closed my eyes and hissed out a breath as her mouth opened, and the warmness encompassed me. I gripped the back of her head, gently pushing her down as she took what she could into the back of her throat.

"Shit, that feels so good," I groaned, making sure I didn't lose control and cum down her throat. "You have to stop, baby. I want to fuck you before I come in your mouth."

She nodded, slowly pulling away as my cock sprung free.

"Fuck, Lia. You have me harder than a fucking rock."

"Well then, I'm scissors."

"What?"

"Rock, paper, scissors. Rock smashes scissors, so get to it."

She chewed her lip playfully as she spread her legs, openly inviting me in.

I lined myself up at her entrance and pushed slowly, giving her pussy time to adjust to my cock. I knew I wasn't abnormally large or anything like that, but Lia was tighter than anyone I'd ever been with, and I didn't want to hurt her.

She cried out as I was fully seated inside of her, her breathing rapid again.

"Slow, deep breaths, baby," I reminded her as I leaned down and kissed her.

Her nails scratched my back as she lifted her hips, sliding me in a little further.

"You're so big," she panted, rocking against me. "I feel so full."

"You're going to be even fuller in a few seconds when I spill all this cum inside you if you don't stop moving," I teased. But seriously, she was going to have me coming right away at this rate.

"This might have to be our *get it out of our system* run, and then we'll do it the right way later."

"The right way?" she questioned, her eyes locking onto mine.

"Where I thoroughly fuck you and make you come repeatedly on my cock."

"Oh."

"For now, I'm just trying not to come yet, but you keep clenching around me, and it's really fucking hard."

"Just do it, Mason. Fuck me real quick and come. We have all day to get this out of our systems."

I nodded, gritting my teeth as I began pumping inside of her. I pulled out and then thrust back in, loving the way she cried out and dug her nails into my back again. My hips moved quickly, short, hard movements that caused her to squeeze tighter around me.

"Fuck!" I cried out as ropes of cum shot out of me and spilled inside the most perfect pussy I had ever fucked.

Twenty-Three
Lia

"Is your leg okay?" Mason asked, shifting beside me.

"I'm still seeing stars. The last thing I'm worried about is my leg," I replied with a giggle as my stomach growled loudly, drawing his attention to that.

"Breakfast is ready. I came to tell you, but then…"

"You decided to fuck me instead?"

"It wasn't my fault. You flashed me your tits and I was a goner."

"You startled me! It wasn't my fault!"

"Says the girl who came out of the bathroom wearing nothing but a towel barely secured. I think you were planning it all along."

I scrunched my face and looked at him. His hair was slightly disheveled from where I had run my fingers through it. Even with the stubble dotting his jawline, he was gorgeous.

"Trust me, if I were planning to seduce you, I would have come out wearing nothing at all."

"Well, that's the house rule from here on out. You are no longer allowed to wear clothes and must be naked 24/7."

"I don't think that will go over well when Jones and Bella come back." I giggled as his fingers wrapped around my waist, tugging me into his side.

"Then come stay with me again. You said it yourself that you slept better in my bed. I have fluffy pillows…"

I inhaled slowly and let it out softly as I thought about it.

"But you'll be going back to work soon and I'm already doing better where I don't need someone helping me all the time."

"No, but that doesn't mean that I won't stop worrying about you."

"Does that mean you kinda like me?" I teased, laughing harder when his fingers tickled my sides.

"I was starting to…"

"But?"

"But then you didn't immediately agree to stay with me so I could continue blowing your mind with my sex-tacular skills in bed."

"Well, I mean, we only got started. Yeah, I had a good orgasm, but who says if you can pull that off again? Technically, I was already all revved up and ready to go. I did all the hard work; you had the easy job."

He fell back on the pillow, closed his eyes, and shook his head.

"Are you denying it?"

"I'm not admitting or denying anything, Lia. But I will say that I would stop talking so much shit if I were you."

"Oh yeah? Why's that?" I popped up on my elbow to look down at him.

"Because if you don't, I'm gonna shove my cock down your throat again to quiet you down. Now get dressed and meet me in the kitchen. You're going to need your energy for what I have planned for you today."

"You're not going to stay and help me?" I asked, kinda baffled by his new attitude as he climbed off the bed and pulled his joggers on.

"You said it yourself, Lia. You don't need my help anymore. If you want me to do things for you, you're gonna have to start working for it."

He turned and walked out the door, leaving me naked and alone on the bed with a grin spread tightly against my cheeks.

By the time I got dressed and hobbled into the kitchen, he was already sitting at the table with two plates of food and cups of coffee ready. I pulled out the chair, sat down, then rested my crutches on the chair beside me.

"Everything looks and smells delicious." I lifted a piece of crispy bacon to my lips and took a bite.

"Thank you. Sorry it's cold. I didn't want to ruin it by trying to reheat it."

"It's okay. Cold food is more than fine with me."

"That's just because you got laid. Old Lia would have been bitching and groaning the second she got hungry and there wasn't food on the table."

I lowered my strip of bacon from my mouth and playfully glared at him.

"Are you insinuating that I'm only in a good mood because you gave me an orgasm?"

"No," he replied around a mouthful of food as he swallowed. "I'm saying you're in a good mood because I gave you an orgasm *and* some dick. Much better than anything you would have gotten with that micro penis."

"*Bullet.*"

"Same difference. My point being that now that I know what makes you happy—or rather in an approachable mood—I can stop walking on eggshells trying to stay on your good side."

"Oh really?"

"Yup. Now eat your breakfast."

"You're so demanding."

"If you only knew." He winked and kept eating his breakfast as if he didn't just send goosebumps all over my skin with the look he gave me.

Once we finished eating, I tried to help clean up in the kitchen, only to get ushered back to the couch, where I was told to take it easy. Even though he said I needed to start doing things on my own, I was able to read between the lines to know he meant the things I could *safely* do on my own. The things I had been too stubborn to let him help me with—like getting dressed.

I was sitting on the couch, trying to find the cooking show we had been watching at his place, but frustrated when I couldn't find it.

"We can go catch up at my house," he offered, sitting next to me as I flipped through the search results. "I have some stuff I need to get done over there anyway."

"What? I thought we had a whole day full of stuff that needed my energy?" I teased.

"We do, but I can do that stuff anywhere. Here. There. Wherever."

"You're giving me *Green Eggs and Ham* vibes."

"Well, if that turns you on," he whispered, leaning in to kiss my neck. "I'll eat you here. I'll eat you there. I'll eat you anywhere. In a house, in a box—"

"Please don't say with a fox," I said with another giggle.

"Definitely not. Sharing is one thing I will *not* be doing."

"Good to know."

"So, what do you say? We go back to my place. I'll put the cooking show on, and we can watch it while I devour your sweet pussy?"

"I say… why is your house so far away? Let's get this party started!"

Twenty-Four
Mason

"There's no way she's going to finish in time," Lia said as I slid her shorts off and tossed them to the side.

"Do you want to race? See who can finish first—you or her?"

She turned and looked at me, her blue eyes glistening with mischief.

"Sounds like the kind of competition I could get on board with."

"Good, because I'm starving, and you're standing between me and my dessert."

"By all means, don't let me stop you."

She leaned back on the couch and let her legs fall open the best she could while keeping her injured foot propped on the pillow I'd set up for her. Her black panties were barely enough to cover her, but that didn't mean I didn't want them off.

"Are you sure about this, Lia?" I asked, hating the way my voice changed with uncertainty, but I couldn't move forward without her consent.

"Yes, I'm more than sure about it. Please don't make me beg for it again."

I chuckled against her thigh as I got situated on the floor, slowly pulling her panties down her legs, careful not to hurt her. She must have shaved this morning in the shower because she was more or less baby-smooth down there, minus a few spots she missed. I would never tell her that, though. I appreciated the effort she made and could tell after breakfast how stiff and sore she was, which, given the long shower she took explained why.

I leaned in, gently kissing her skin as I worked my way to where I really wanted to be. Her fingers grabbed my hair, pulling hard as my mouth hovered over her pussy, my warm breath tickling her skin.

A small gasp escaped her lips as I ran my tongue along her lips, my finger gently sliding in and spreading her wetness. I loved how easily Lia got aroused for me but hated how I almost immediately got a raging hard on. It wouldn't be a problem if I were planning to just plow into her, but I was determined to take my time and bring her all the pleasure I could.

I slipped another finger inside, pumping slowly as I took my time licking and sucking her clit. She was already on the verge of coming, but I wanted to really draw it out and make it the best fucking orgasm she ever had.

"How much time does she have?" I asked, pulling away for a split second before sucking her clit again.

"Two minutes," she replied, her breathing already getting labored.

"I can get you there in under one."

She moaned and pulled my hair harder as I flicked my tongue against her clit, making her thighs tremble. Knowing she was getting close, I changed the position of my fingers, making sure they were hitting her g-spot and began applying the pressure I knew she needed. My mouth focused on sucking her clit as I placed my other hand on her lower stomach and pressed down, knowing the additional pressure would help get her there.

"Fuck," she cried out, her thighs immediately trying to lock closed on my head. "No, Mason, I can't. I'm going to pee!"

"You're not, baby. I promise. Try to relax and keep breathing for me. Lots of quick breaths this time."

"Okay."

I could hear her panting and knew she was on the edge but wouldn't get there if she didn't stop overthinking things in her head. I pulled my fingers out and focused on her clit, knowing that would be the easiest way to get her to come.

A few seconds later, she cried out and screamed my name as her pussy spasmed against my mouth.

In the background, I heard the guy on TV announce they were down to their last sixty seconds. I grinned, knowing I beat them and that I was slowly building her trust in believing I could get her to come when I said I would.

****

Lia and I spent the day binge-watching reality cooking shows, and then we stopped so I could make dinner. She insisted on helping, so I set her up at the island where she could sit on a stool and cut the veggies for the salad after I washed them. She had mentioned earlier that she had a craving for steak and baked potatoes, which was what we were now having. Whatever Lia wanted, I made sure Lia got.

"So, where did you learn to cook?" she asked, looking up as she dumped a handful of chopped cucumbers into the bowl.

"I don't really know. I grew up knowing the basics and could cook basic stuff, but I think my obsession with cooking shows has really helped me level up my skills."

"That makes sense. I mean, I haven't cooked in who knows how long—but I'm happy to say that my julienned carrots are top-notch."

"They are quite impressive," I agreed, leaning over to look into the bowl filled with vibrant colors. "How do you like your steak?"

"Medium-well, please."

"You got it. I'm going to run these out to the grill real quick."

I grabbed the tray of meat and headed outside, making sure to keep the door open so I could hear if Lia needed anything. Just as I was setting the meat on the grill, I heard a loud curse word and looked up to find Lia trying to get up without her crutches.

"What are you doing? What's wrong?" I asked as I rushed in to find blood pouring out of her finger.

"Son of a bitch," she hissed, looking around the counter. "I need a paper towel."

I reached over and grabbed the roll from the counter, unwinding it as I wrapped a few around her finger.

"Are you okay?"

"Yeah, I got distracted and accidentally cut myself. I didn't realize how sharp the knife is."

I applied more pressure, frowning when the paper towel immediately turned red, already soaked with her blood. I needed to see how deep the cut was and if she needed stitches, but I wanted to try to stop the bleeding first.

I grabbed a few more paper towels and wrapped them around the blood-soaked ones, then lifted her wrist to be elevated above her heart and held it there. I gently pushed her back to the stool so she could sit down and not have to worry about her foot on top of everything else.

"Always here to save me," she whispered, her blue eyes clouding with tears.

"You say that like it's a bad thing."

"Well, I mean, I don't *love* getting hurt, but I guess it's not such a terrible thing that you're always there to take care of me. I am sorry that I seem to be so accident-prone lately."

"I don't love that you keep getting hurt, either. Trust me, I would rather be *taking care* of you in other ways. But this—this I don't mind. You're not a burden by any means, Lia, so please don't allow yourself to feel like you are."

I looked down and studied her finger. The bleeding appeared to have stopped, so I gently removed the paper towels and carefully examined the cut. It was bad, but thankfully, it didn't look like it needed stitches.

"I'm going to grab the first aid kit," I said, gently laying her hand on the island. "We'll need to wash it out first, but I don't want you trying to do anything until I come back," I added when I noticed her trying to reach for her crutches.

"I appreciate the concern, but you return to work in a few days. I have to be able to do things on my own. It's just going to the sink and washing my finger. I'll be okay, and you'll be back in a minute if I need anything."

I nodded, not sure what else to say because she was right. Even though I hated it, I did have to go back to work soon and wouldn't be able to spend my time here watching over her.

<u>Twenty-Five</u>
Lia

"This is heaven," I said, cuddling into the pillows on Mason's bed.

"I've been known to have a way to get women into my bed, but I never thought it would be my pillows," he said with a laugh.

"It's not just the pillows." I looked up at him with a flirty smile on my face and batted my lashes.

"Oh really?" He reached back and pulled his shirt over his head, revealing the most glorious six-pack that I loved to admire.

"Nope. It's also the pillowtop mattress."

"Is that it?"

I nodded.

"You sure there isn't *anything* else about this bed that makes it *heaven*?" He crawled across it and stalked toward me.

"Can't think of anything…."

He grabbed my sides and tickled them as his mouth found my neck and bit lightly into the skin right below my ear.

"Maybe this will jar your memory," he growled, pressing his erection against my thigh.

"That's a start," I panted.

"Well then, I guess it's a good thing that I know how to finish what I start."

I closed my eyes and enjoyed the feel of his lips as they explored my neck, working their way down to my breasts. He pulled my tank top down before sucking my nipple into his mouth, earning a moan in response.

My fingers gripped his hair, my body already lighting up for him as every nerve ending came to life. I had been with my fair share of guys—well, probably more than anyone's fair share—but no one had ever been able to bring my body to life the way Mason did. I used to think sex was just sex and foreplay was overrated, but that was before I learned that I had been doing it wrong this whole time.

He continued to work his way down my body, my legs spreading willingly for him as he lowered himself between them and began teasing my clit with his tongue through the thin fabric of my panties.

"There is one rule you have to follow if you want to sleep in my bed," he mumbled against my thigh.

"Oh yeah? What's that?"

"You're not allowed to wear panties."

"Deal."

I squirmed beneath his touch as he worked to get them off.

"Better yet—you don't get to wear anything to bed. I want you completely naked beside me."

"Alright, but only if you agree to fuck me every time he gets hard."

"I don't know if either of us will ever get any sleep at that rate, Lia. You have him hard 24/7."

"Then I guess it's my job to take care of that."

He tossed my panties to the floor and then went back to working my clit with his tongue while using two fingers to fuck me until I came on his tongue.

I couldn't wait for my leg to be better so I could climb on top of him and ride him the way I wanted to. But for now, I was more than happy to sit back and let Mason fuck me into oblivion.

We fell asleep shortly after that, and for once, it felt like everything in my life was right as I cuddled against him and fell into the best sleep that I'd had in a long time.

****

The sun was peering through the curtains when I woke up, showering the room in a warm glow. I reached over and found the other side of the bed empty, then heard the shower running. I grabbed my phone from the nightstand, checking the time, when I noticed a message from Kensy.

Kensy: Hey! We're back in town—technically, we got back last night, but it was super late, and I didn't want to wake you. We have some unpacking to do, but I thought maybe you and I could go to lunch and catch up. Tipsy Taquito at noon? My treat!

A grin spread across my face, excited to see my best friend and hear all about her trip.

Me: Welcome back! I would love to! Mason is in the shower, but I can check with him to see if he can drop me off.

Kensy: I can come pick you up. I don't mind.

Me: Are you sure?

Kensy: Absolutely! I'll text you when I'm on my way.

Me: Sounds good! See you in a few hours!

I put my phone down as the bathroom door opened, and Mason walked out with a towel hung low around his hips. My eyes immediately left his and traveled down the length of his body to the bulge protruding beneath the fabric.

"Everything alright?" he asked coyly, leaning against the doorframe as if my body wasn't suddenly on fire and about to combust.

"It will be once you bring that cock over here."

His eyebrow arched playfully as he pushed off the wall.

"You mean this one?" He undid the towel, letting it fall to the floor.

He reached down and grabbed his cock, slowly running his hand up and down the length.

I nodded, continuing to watch as he played with himself, taking painfully slow steps to get to me. Once he was close enough, I leaned over and grabbed him, swatting his hands away as I took him into mine.

"I can't wait until I'm better so I can ride this," I muttered, licking my lips before taking him into my mouth.

He hissed and grabbed a handful of my hair as I took him deeper to the back of my throat. I relaxed my jaw and allowed myself a moment to work past gagging before I slowly moved up and down his length.

"We can figure out a way," he said, confusing me as I already forgot what we were talking about. "For you to ride me. But if you don't stop sucking my cock, I'm going to come before you get the chance."

With one hand still stroking him, I lowered my other between my legs and began rubbing my clit. I needed to get off and now. The harder I sucked him, the faster I rubbed. His grunting and groaning only spurred me on, and soon, I was pulsating around my fingers as my orgasm crashed over me along with ropes of cum that shot down my throat.

I slowly pulled him out of my mouth, making sure to lick every last drop off.

"You're going to be the death of me," he said with a shake of his head. "I guess we'll have to add you riding me to the agenda today."

"Sounds like a plan," I replied with a laugh. "But I do have lunch plans if that's okay?"

He frowned, confusion playing across his face.

"Why wouldn't it be okay?"

I shrugged, not knowing how to explain that I was worried he might have had other plans for us. Plus, it felt like something a boyfriend and girlfriend would talk about, but we weren't that. I didn't know what we were and that left me feeling weird that I didn't know how to navigate stuff like this between us.

"I don't know. I just didn't know what the plan was for today."

He sat down on the edge of the bed beside me.

"I didn't have any other than getting caught up on some housework before I go back to work tomorrow. Oh, and fucking you a few times. Other than that, the day is wide open."

"Oh. Okay." I nodded as if that gave me the clarity I needed.

"But Lia?"

"Yeah?"

"You don't have to worry about asking permission to do whatever you want. I like having you stay here, but I don't have any expectations around that. I want you to feel comfortable being here and knowing that you're free to make decisions for yourself."

"I am comfortable here. I guess it's just kinda weird because I don't know what exactly this thing is between us."

I let out a shaky breath and watched as something registered on his face.

"I mean, I'm not trying to make you uncomfortable or anything. And I don't need a label for whatever this is—I just—"

"I like you a lot, Lia. And I think given what we've been doing with each other, I would feel better knowing that we're exclusive."

"So, you're like, my boyfriend?" I asked hesitantly.

"If that's what you want to call it, yes."

"What do you want to call it?"

"Well, if I had it my way, I would label myself as the best cock you've ever had and guaranteed orgasm giver. Sounds so much better than just *boyfriend*."

"That's kind of a mouthful," I teased. "Maybe I should just stick with boyfriend?"

"You do pretty well with handling a mouthful, but yes, we can stick with boyfriend. Your brother is going to kick my ass anyway when he finds out about us. It's probably best that you don't try to introduce me as the guy who's giving you good cock."

"The *best* cock," I corrected. "And don't worry, I can handle my brother."

Twenty-Six
Lia

"Oh my God, I've missed Tipsy Taquito," Kensy said as she pushed a tortilla chip smothered in guacamole into her mouth. "Don't get me wrong, everything we had in California was great, but nothing—and I mean nothing—will ever compare to this guacamole."

"I think the whole town knows about your love of guacamole," I teased, taking a bite of my food.

"True, but the one thing I don't know about is what in the world is going on with you."

"What do you mean?" I frowned and tilted my head.

"Since when do you eat salad? I thought for sure they got the order wrong and might have assumed Bella was joining us, so they just brought it out randomly. But then no other food came, and you're actually eating it."

I shrugged and tried not to laugh at the look of disgust on her face as I shoved a giant forkful of lettuce and meat into my mouth.

"Seriously, I go away for a few days and you turn into someone new."

"You were gone almost two weeks," I countered with a laugh. "And I'm just trying to eat better. Mason has been cooking for us, and I've felt a lot better not eating out all the time. Thought I would try something new."

"I'm sure you're trying lots of *new* things. I swear I haven't seen you smile this much in—I don't even know how long. Ever? Have you ever smiled?" Kensy leaned forward playfully, narrowing her eyes to try to find it.

"Shut up, or I'm going to throw your guacamole in the trash."

"You wouldn't!" she gasped, clutching one hand to her chest as she used the other to pull the bowl closer to her.

"I'm a changed woman, Kensy. There's no limit to what I wouldn't do."

"I guess I'm going to have to talk with Mason and see if he can factory reset you or something."

She winked but then ducked as I tossed a tortilla chip at her head.

"I'm just kidding. I don't know what's gotten into you—I mean, I'm pretty sure I know *who*—but I like this new side of you. It's very refreshing."

"Thanks. It's been an interesting week, to say the least."

"How's your ankle?"

"As good as I can expect. Mason has taken good care of me and has basically given me my own private home health care, so I can't complain about that. But I still have at least another four weeks in this cast, and then I'll have to do physical therapy."

"So," she said, then paused to pop a chip into her mouth. "What exactly is going on with you and Mason? I have to admit, it's incredibly strange not to hear you call him Dr. Dickhead. Did you seriously go from full-on hating him to loving him in the blink of an eye?"

I chewed slowly, biding my time as I considered my answer. Mason and I had just talked about it this morning, so it wasn't like I shouldn't call him my boyfriend, yet my mouth had the hardest time getting the word out.

"I don't know that I would say that I full-on hated him before," I replied, testing the words as they came.

"Lia, you said you would rather chew your arm off and beat yourself senseless with it than to ever be stuck in a room with him again. I think that borders on full-on hate."

"Maybe I was being dramatic." I sighed and let my fork drop to my plate.

"Since when are you not dramatic?" my brother asked, scaring the shit out of me as he slid into the booth beside Kensy.

"Holy shit! What are you doing here?" I held my hand to my chest and glared at him. "I thought this was supposed to be girl time for me and Kensy?"

"Relax," he replied, holding his hand up to stop me. "I'm not staying. I just came to grab some food and then I'm heading over to Mom and Dad's since they're babysitting. I knew you guys would be here, so I thought I would come over and say hi to my sister, whom I haven't seen in a few days."

"It's been closer to two weeks," I corrected, rolling my eyes.

"And obviously, a lot can change in a short time. Since when do you eat salad?"

I tossed my hands in the air and shook my head at them.

"I eat salad!"

"Since when?" he asked, the corners of his lips curling up as he watched me get riled up.

"Since always."

"Pretending you're making a salad by putting different colored candies in a bowl and mixing them around doesn't count as salad." He pointed a finger at me.

"You're the worst," I grunted, kicking my good foot under the table, hoping to make contact with his leg.

"Ouch!" Kensy yelped, shifting quickly in the booth to avoid being the target again.

"Sorry." I looked down, tore off a small piece of the tortilla shell, and popped it in my mouth.

"Well, they just called my number, so I gotta go. But it was good to see you, Lia. Stop acting so weird—I don't like it. Do you want me to order you something with more carbs before I go?"

I glared at him as he stood up.

"Leave her alone. She was just getting ready to tell me what's been going on in her life since we've been gone until you came over and interrupted," Kensy said, looking up adoringly at him.

"You can fill me in later," he replied, leaning down to kiss her. "Don't forget to bring some guacamole home for later."

"Eeew," I muttered, shaking my head. "Stop being gross."

"Stop being weird. Eat a taco or two. You're more crabby when you just eat salad. I don't even know what to do with you right now." He bopped me on the head and walked off to get his to-go order.

"Okay, so now that your brother is gone, you were saying that you never really hated Dr. Dickhead, you just kinda hated him? Is that it?"

"I don't know. It's so hard to explain. It's like I used to think I hated him and never wanted anything to do with him, but then once I was forced to spend all this time with him, I found he's not as bad as I thought. I mean, we've been stuck together for over a week, and he's been nothing but nice to me. Maybe I just misjudged him until now."

"Would you say that you might have come to *love* him?"

The color drained from my face so quickly I had to brace myself in the booth to keep from getting dizzy. That wasn't a word I had allowed myself to entertain because I knew what would happen if I did.

"I don't think that's what *this* is at all. I mean, we don't need to have actual names for everything or obsess over what it is or isn't. I just know that I like him now, and he likes me. That's all there is to it. Nothing that needs to get all complicated and—"

"Lia?"

"Yeah?"

"I hate to break it to you, but you're rambling on like someone who's in love and doesn't want to admit it."

I opened my mouth and then snapped it shut.

"I…"

"But…"

"You know it seems like it, but…"

"Fuck."

Kensy reached her hands up in an attempt to cover the smile spreading across her face but failed to hide it.

"Oh my GOD! My best friend is finally in love!"

"Shhhh! Would you be quiet?" I hissed, looking around to make sure no one heard her.

"Why? I'm freaking excited about it! This is a wonderful thing, Lia."

"I never said I was in *love* with him. You just decided it on your own and now you're trying to force me to get on board with it and shouting it to the world before I even know how I feel."

"How does he feel?" she asked, ignoring my rant.

"About you telling people that I love him? I don't know. Knowing him, he's probably smiling, thinking he's won another round with me."

"So you don't think he would be upset to know that you love him?"

"I never said that, Kensy. You're putting words into my mouth."

"And you're having a terrible time denying them."

I inhaled deeply and slowly let it out through pursed lips as I considered that. I *hadn't* said that I loved him, but I also hadn't said that I *didn't* either. It was impossible to know how I felt when the conversation about feelings literally just came up today. It wasn't like I'd had time to think about it or gather my thoughts.

"I hit him in the head with the mini bullet Bella gave me before she left," I said, changing the subject, knowing that Kensy would be easily distracted by the story.

Her jaw dropped as her brows furrowed in confusion.

"You what?"

I lowered my voice so no one else could hear as I got into the dirty details of what happened.

"I was trying to get some relief while he was out picking up dinner and didn't expect him to come back so soon. He walked in on me, and I panicked and threw it at him, hitting him in the forehead."

"Oh my God!" Kensy shrieked, covering her mouth as a snort came through with her laughter. "What did he say?"

"Well, he was very confused for a while."

"Like you gave him a concussion from it? Dear Lord, how heavy was that thing?"

"No, he was fine. He had like a tiny bruise and that was it."

"What was he confused about then?"

"He couldn't figure out what women like about it and was convinced that I had something for micro penises."

"I don't get it," she said, shaking her head.

"He thought that I used that tiny thing to fuck myself with until I explained that it's just for clitoral stimulation. Then he had the nerve to ask why I didn't just have my partner do it for me instead of using the toy."

"What did you tell him?" Kensy leaned forward, resting her elbows on the table, fully invested now.

"I told him that I didn't have a partner and that every guy I'd been with before either hadn't bothered to try to get me off or they genuinely didn't know how."

"Oh my gosh!! Please, please, please tell me that he took this as the opportunity to be the hands-on teacher to show you all the ways he could make you come!" she squealed, stomping her feet on the floor.

"I mean, not at first...."

Her eyes widened as my cheeks grew redder and flamed with embarrassment.

"Lia!!!!"

"What?" I laughed nervously, looking around to see if her loud noises were drawing attention to us again. Thankfully, everyone seemed too busy eating to care about the dirty stuff we were talking about over lunch.

"You are being such a tease with withholding all of the dirty details about what happened!"

"We're in the middle of a restaurant," I hissed, looking around pointedly to prove my point.

"And that's never stopped you before. Remember that time when you went into graphic detail to Bella and Me about how that guy from your pharmacology class went down on you during a study session, but then he was trying to multitask and kept stopping to ask you questions about possible side effects for each drug you talked about?"

"Oh my God, don't remind me." I covered my face with my hands, shuddering as I remembered in horrid detail. That was the first time I had actually gotten close to coming with a guy, and he kept ruining it by stopping right before I could come and then making me work for it all over again. By the fourth time, I was pissed off and over it, so I kicked him out and refused to talk to him ever again.

"I'm just saying—you're always willing to spill the beans and give us the explicit details of your love life until now."

"So, what's your point?"

"That maybe you should stop and ask yourself why. If this really is just a quick fling between you guys, then why aren't you treating him the way you've treated all of your other flings?"

I looked around the room, more so to distract myself from answering the question.

"He said he wants to be exclusive," I blurted out, finally bringing my attention back to Kensy.

Her eyes widened as her smile spread across her face again.

"So he's not just a fling, he's your boyfriend?"

I nodded and finally allowed myself to smile, too.

"Yeah, he's my boyfriend."

Twenty-Seven

Mason

"How was lunch?" I asked as I held the door open for Lia after Kensy dropped her off.

"It was good. I got the taco salad, and then everyone judged me for it."

"Why?" I asked, a soft laughter floating out.

"Apparently, I'm not a very healthy eater around my friends and family," she said with a shrug as she stepped inside and headed toward the couch. "My brother demanded that I eat more carbs and said I was crabbier when I just ate salad. I think *he* was the crabby one."

"Did you tell him about us?" I moved her crutches out of the way and sat beside her, loving how she automatically leaned into me as I wrapped my arm around her shoulders.

She shook her head.

"No, but I did tell Kensy, and that's as good as telling him because she'll spill the news as soon as she gets home."

"Yeah? What did she say?"

"She was confused how I could go so quickly from hating you to lov—"

Her body stiffened beside me as her words immediately stopped.

I chewed my lower lip and debated whether to let this slide and change the topic or to keep pushing and see if I could get more out of her.

"How you could go so quickly from hating me to what? Sorry, you cut off at the end."

"You know what the rest of the sentence was."

"I don't, actually, because you didn't finish saying it. And believe me, I would hate to accidentally put words in your mouth."

"I seriously doubt that you would hate it. You're so willing to put everything else in there."

She was acting bratty, which I knew meant she was feeling defensive. About what—I wasn't sure yet. It could be that talking about love and whether she was feeling it for me was too much for her to handle right now, but something told me it was more than that, and I was determined to get to the root cause of this *tantrum*.

"Are you going to keep being a brat, or are we going to have an open and honest conversation?"

"Depends on what you want to talk about."

"You know what I want to talk about, Lia."

"Fine, then I guess I'll continue to be a *brat*, as you call it."

"Have it your way," I sighed, getting up off the couch.

Her eyes narrowed as she watched me.

"So, what? That's it? I won't talk about what you want to so you're just going to walk away from me? Who's being a brat now? Throwing a fit because you didn't get your way?"

I reached back and pulled my shirt over my head and then tossed it to the floor.

"I never said I was walking away. You assumed what you wanted. I was just getting comfortable before we began."

"Begin what?"

"The exorcism to get that attitude out of you."

She opened her mouth to say something but snapped it shut as I reached down and grabbed her good leg, yanking her body until she was lying on the couch instead of sitting.

"You run your mouth so much and let that attitude get the better of you, but it's okay. I know how to fix it now. I know you're not hangry because you just had lunch— though your brother might be onto something with the extra carbs needed to make you less grumpy," I teased.

"Don't you dare tell my brother he's right about anything, or I'll murder you in your sleep."

"Why not? Gotta find something to get on his good side to keep him from killing me when he finds out that I've been fucking this attitude out of you. I mean, I'd like to think that I'm doing community service here because everyone benefits when you're back to being nice again. It's not like I mind the extra work or anything either."

"Wow, way to make me feel so special, *Dr. Dickhead.*"

I reached up and hooked my fingers into the waistband of her shorts, pausing before taking them off.

"Can I?"

"What are you going to do if I say no? Convince the town that I'm in a shitty mood because you couldn't cure me with a quickie?"

"If you say no, I will respect your word and won't push you to do anything, Lia. I need you to always understand that. I don't care how bad either of us wants something. If you change your mind and no longer want it, we immediately stop."

The tone in my voice changed drastically, sobering both of us up from the playful—yet somewhat combative—manner we were in just a few seconds ago.

"It's fine, Mason. You can take them off. I would say panties, too, but I didn't wear any this morning."

Heat rushed through my veins at the thought of her being out in public with those short shorts on and nothing underneath.

"Are you fucking kidding me, Lia?"

"You know what, never mind. We don't have to do this. Hell, it was your idea to begin with, but—"

"I mean, are you fucking kidding me that you wore this outfit out without panties?"

My dick strained against my pants, already aching for a release. My fingers brushed against her skin, leaving goosebumps prickling along it.

She nodded and chewed her bottom lip, the playful and bratty side returning.

"Do you know how easy it would have been for someone to see up your shorts and get a full view of this beautiful pussy?"

"You mean like this?"

She opened her legs and let them fall to the sides, her shorts moving slightly as her lips glistened from her arousal.

"This is *my* pussy now, Lia. Remember that. I'm the only one who gets to see it, feel it, or taste it. It's mine. You wear shorts like that without panties again, and I'll bend you over my knee and turn that ass red."

"Is that a promise or a threat, *Dr. Dickhead?*"

"Everything I say is a promise. Never forget that. Now can I take your fucking shorts off?"

She nodded and lifted her butt as I pulled them down her legs.

"You've been such a naughty girl this afternoon, Lia," I said quietly, shaking my head as I got to my knees and kneeled in front of the couch. "You're gonna have to pay for that."

Before she could say anything, I lowered my mouth to her pussy and began licking mercilessly. She cried out and arched her back as she reached for my head. I loved the way she pulled my hair when she got close to coming, the pain a welcome dose of ecstasy.

I could feel her body responding so quickly to me, her thighs shaking around my head as she got closer to coming. Just when she was on the verge, I pulled back and stopped.

Her eyes flew open as she stared at me in disbelief.

"What are you doing? Why did you stop? I didn't come yet."

"I know. Trust me, Lia, I know your body well enough to know when you're about to."

"Okay, so then why didn't you let me? I was almost there," she whined, reaching her hand down to finish what I started.

I grabbed it and stopped her before climbing over her body and pinning both arms above her head.

"Naughty girls don't get to come until I say so," I whispered in her ear, loving the way her body felt beneath mine, with her chest rising and falling heavily against me.

"That's not fair."

"No, but was it fair that you wore those shorts out in public, knowing someone might see something that you agreed was mine this morning?"

I waited for her to respond, loving the flush of color on her cheeks as she tried to regulate her breathing.

"I didn't think so. So, that's what happens when you act out, baby. I'll do my best to fix this attitude of yours, but there's going to be some punishment along the way."

"You're so mean."

"But you like it. Look at how wet you are already for me. The more I talk, the wetter you get. And you know I'm going to take care of you when *I'm* ready to. You'll come so hard that you won't be able to see straight."

"Promises, promises."

"More of the bratty attitude? That's okay. I know how to deal with that."

"Then do it." She let out a deep, frustrated breath, blowing a piece of hair out of her face as I continued to hold her arms above her head.

"Fine."

I reached down and undid my pants, pulling my cock free. Without any warning, I lined it up at her soaking-wet entrance and plunged inside.

"Ahhhh!" she cried out, her body immediately curving into mine as she tried to wrap her legs around me to keep me inside her. "Fucckkkk."

"First, I'm going to start with fucking some of this attitude out, and then we'll get back to the punishments." I pulled out all the way and then slammed inside her, again and again, loving how I hit the spot that I knew drove her crazy.

She moaned and tried to lift her hips to meet my thrusts, but the way I was pinning her down limited her movements. I knew that she was going to come in seconds with the way my cock was lined up inside her. Her breathing was quick and labored as she climbed that mountain, only to have me rip it all away. I quickly changed positions, feeling her thighs tighten in a death grip around me.

"You fucker," she growled. "You knew I was almost there."

"And I told you I would let you come when I was ready for you to," I replied, gritting my teeth to keep from exploding inside of her.

"Why don't we just forget about the games and just do what we do best?"

"It's a little too late for that, baby. You started this, I'll finish it."

"Finish me, and I'll be all set. You won't hear another word out of me today."

"As much fun as that sounds, I think I'll stick with my original plan."

I let go of her wrists and gripped her hips, steadying myself as I fucked her hard and fast until I emptied my load inside of her.

"At least someone got to come," she said bitterly as I hung my head, struggling to catch my breath before I pulled out.

"Stop being a baby. You'll come soon enough."

"I wouldn't have to complain if you'd just give in and—"

Her words stopped, replaced by a sharp gasp as I pulled out and immediately began rubbing her clit with two fingers.

"Yes," she moaned, her eyes fluttering closed and legs spreading open for me. "Please, Mason. Don't torture me anymore. Just let me come already."

I didn't worry about the mess already leaking out of her because I was about to make an even bigger one.

Standing above her, I removed my fingers from her clit and pushed them inside, making sure they hit her G-spot. I could already tell she was going to fight me on another missed orgasm, but was relieved when she relaxed and allowed me to pleasure her body. I took my time, making my movements slow and deliberate with enough pressure for it to feel good for her.

When she started squirming, I could tell she was almost there.

"Mason, I have to pee," she whispered.

"You don't baby. And if you do, it's okay. Just relax and let me make you come."

"But you're not even touching my clit. How are you going to make me come? There's all this pressure, and I really feel like I need to use the bathroom."

"It's supposed to feel that way. Just trust me, okay?"

She nodded and closed her eyes, relaxing into my touch as I placed my other hand on her lower stomach and began increasing the speed and pressure I applied to her G-spot with my fingers. I could hear her breathing change and felt her body as it tightened around me.

"Don't fight it, baby," I coaxed. "I promise it's going to feel incredible once you let it happen."

"But, I can't. I can't do it."

"Yes, you can. Deep breaths, Lia. Relax for me, and let your body do what it wants to. Stop fighting it and give me this orgasm."

"I… I…" she panted.

She was so close, and I wasn't going to stop until I got her there and sent her over the edge. I fucked her quicker with my fingers, making sure to keep hitting the same spot while I pressed down hard with my hand to maximize the pressure.

A few seconds later, Lia was screaming my name as she came, her body shaking beneath me as she came down from it.

"Oh my God, I did pee!"

Her eyes fluttered open, looking down in shocked horror.

"No, baby. You didn't pee. You squirted, and it was fucking amazing."

"Oh," she whispered, still out of breath as she let herself fall back to the pillow and closed her eyes. "I didn't know I could do that."

Twenty- Eight
Lia

I sat cuddled against Mason's chest, drawing circles up and down his arm as we watched another episode of the reality cooking show. I was full, relaxed, and felt incredible after the most intense orgasm I'd ever had before.

"She's so pretty," I said softly, nodding to the single mom who was out-cooking every chef and making it look like a piece of cake. She wasn't even sweating as she plated her food minutes before the timer.

"You're so pretty," he replied, kissing the side of my head. "I can see that someone is back to being in a good mood again. Glad I could fix that for you."

"I gotta admit, there's not much I could complain about right now. Nothing to be in a bad mood over."

"Good. That's what I like to hear."

He squeezed me gently, but it felt like the world's biggest hug.

"Can I ask you a question?" I asked, lifting my head to look back at him.

"Of course."

"I don't mean this in a rude way because it is actually a turn-on, but why do you always obsess over making sure

I tell you that I'm okay with sex stuff before it happens? I mean, we're officially boyfriend and girlfriend now, so I guess it just feels like it should be a given."

"Just because we're dating doesn't mean that I will ever assume I have your consent, Lia. No is always a complete sentence, regardless of the circumstances. Just because you're my girlfriend doesn't give me access to you unless you want it right then and there. You should always demand that level of respect for yourself, no matter who or what it is."

"You're very passionate about this," I said cautiously, turning the best I could so I could see him face to face.

He nodded but looked at the TV as his jaw tightened.

"When I was in college, there was a situation with this girl, and it changed my life forever."

I pulled my head back slightly, trying to mask the surprise so he'd continue telling his story.

"I grew up in a small town, even smaller than this one, and as you can imagine, everyone knew everything about everything. Jess and I had been friends for a few years, but nothing more than that because she had a boyfriend. One night, I was at a party with some of my friends. It was the end of the semester, and we all needed to burn off some steam. I had a few drinks but didn't want to get drunk since that wasn't really my thing. Soon, a crowd gathered where I was, and a bonfire started. Jess and some of her girlfriends joined us, and I didn't think anything of it when she sat beside me because that was just how things were back home."

He lifted his shoulders and let out a long, heavy breath.

"Jess and I got to talking, and she asked me if I was excited to get into medical school. She was a few years younger than me, and it felt nice being able to brag about all of my accomplishments because I was proud of how far I had come. I didn't think anything of it when she kept getting me another beer until I realized I was a little more than buzzed. Soon, the others left to go play beer pong, and it was just me and Jess at the bonfire."

I had a terrible feeling about where this story was going, but I gave him my full attention as he continued to tell it.

"Before I could process what was happening, Jess had climbed onto my lap and was kissing me. I was delayed in reacting because of the alcohol and didn't think about it until I remembered she was with Brandon. I told her we needed to stop and gently tried to push her off of me. Even if she was okay with cheating on her boyfriend, I wasn't okay with being a willing participant in it. She told me that they had broken up and that she had had a crush on me for years. I couldn't think straight, so I had no idea when the last time I saw them together was. I wanted to make sure I was doing the right thing, but her words were so convincing as she promised me over and over that she was single.

Even in my buzzed state, I knew that nothing should happen between us because she had been drinking, too. I didn't want either of us to do something we would later regret. If she was interested in me, we could circle back around to things once we were both clear-headed. She had a short skirt on and had reached down to stroke me through my pants. I kept telling her we needed to stop, but she didn't want to listen, so I stood up and turned to sit her in the chair beside me. A friend of hers walked up at that moment, and from what I heard later, it looked like I was trying to take advantage of her instead of the other way around."

"Oh no," I whispered, covering my mouth.

"I walked away and headed straight for my dorm, too foggy-headed to be in any position to try to figure things out. The next morning, my phone had blown up with text messages and voicemails about how I had assaulted Jess the night before. I thought I had done the right thing by walking away, but apparently, it just made me look guilty. I found out that Jess hadn't broken up with Brandon and that she lied and said that I was forcing myself onto her instead of it being the other way around."

"Oh my, God, Mason! That's terrible! I'm so sorry."

"The worst part was that the gossip spread so fast I couldn't get ahead of it to tell my side of the story. The school I had just gotten accepted into for med school changed their mind and denied my application. Aside from my parents, no one else believed me. Jess was considered the good girl, the pastor's daughter—the one who could do no wrong. I wasn't a bad kid or anything like that, but I also stayed out of the gossip mill as often as I could. But it turns out that even keeping your head down in a small town doesn't help anyone to rally for you when you need it. Instead, they just figure they never really knew what a monster you really were."

I shook my head and squeezed my arm around his waist.

"I applied to several different med school programs and finally decided Beaumont Creek was where I wanted to go. I packed up and left my life behind me without ever looking back."

"That's so crazy. I can't believe no one would even let you tell your side of the story. And you didn't even do anything wrong."

"I know. But it was a lesson I learned quickly, and I'll never forget. That's why I didn't want to do anything the night we had been drinking, and that's why I'll always make sure you want whatever is happening between us. Even if you say no to something, Lia, that won't change things between us. I will always respect your wishes."

"And I'll respect yours."

"Well, with that said, I have a question of my own for you," he said, raising an eyebrow at me. "Why did you leave the house without any panties today?"

I swallowed loudly and rubbed my lips together nervously.

"I ran out of clean ones and didn't have time to do laundry before Kensy came to pick me up."

He tossed his head back and groaned.

"For the love of God, Lia. Just tell me that you need clean clothes and I'll wash them for you. But please do not ever leave this house without wearing underwear again."

"You got it."

He pulled me into his chest and cuddled me as my phone dinged from the coffee table with a new text message. He reached over, grabbed it, then handed it to me.

Kensy: Hey, your brother wants to know if you guys want to have dinner with us tonight.

I read the message a few times, making sure I was reading it right.

Me: He just saw me this afternoon when he harassed me about not eating enough carbs and judging my taco salad.

Kensy: I know, but he wants to have dinner.

Me: With me and you?

Kensy: You know what I mean.

I swallowed hard and then looked up at Mason, who was invested in the TV and hadn't been reading the messages on my phone. He looked down at me curiously, probably wondering why all the color had suddenly drained from my face.

"What's wrong?"

"My brother wants to meet you."

Twenty- Nine
Mason

I couldn't figure out why Lia was so nervous about having dinner with her brother and Kensy, but she changed her outfit at least fifteen times before deciding on a baggy t-shirt and a pair of jeans.

"What are you wearing?" I asked, leaning against the door frame as I watched her struggle to see herself in the mirror.

"Jeans and a T-shirt."

"Why? It's like a thousand degrees outside. You're going to melt in that. Why don't you wear the shorts and tank top you had on fifteen outfits ago?"

"Because I don't need my brother to think that I'm dressing up all sexy for you," she breathed out, sounding frustrated.

I covered my mouth with my hand as a chuckle slipped out.

"Well, while I do find you undeniably sexy in shorts and a tank top, it's not like you're showing up in a see-through bra and crotchless panties. I *think* he will be fine and will assume you're just wearing regular clothes that everyone else is wearing in this heat."

She stopped for a moment and considered it before yanking her shirt over her head and throwing it at me.

"You're right. I'm already dying of heat."

"Here, let me help you," I offered, gently pushing her back to the bed. I undid her jeans and slid them down her legs before she sat down, making sure not to hurt her foot. Thankfully, she was finally calming down and allowed me to assist her with getting the other outfit on.

"You ready?"

"Yeah. I told Kensy we would meet them at Surf 'N Shack at six. They needed an early night so they could get home and take care of some stuff."

"Sounds good to me."

I helped lead her out of the house and then into the car, the drive there awkwardly quiet as she chewed her nails nervously.

"It's going to be alright, you know?" I asked, gently squeezing her hand to get her attention.

"Yeah. I just, ugh, I've never introduced anyone to my family before. I mean, this morning I woke up happy and thoroughly fucked, then we agreed to be boyfriend and girlfriend, and now it hasn't even been a full twenty-four hours of us being in a committed relationship, and you're meeting my brother, who very well might try to kill you when he knows that—"

"Breathe, Lia. You're going to pass out if you don't stop talking and breathe between sentences. If things are moving too fast, that's fine. I totally get it. Just let me know what you need, and I'll make it happen. If you don't feel like having dinner with them tonight, I'll gladly call and tell them you're not feeling well."

"No," she said with a sigh, finally taking some oxygen into her body. "It's fine. It can't be that bad, can it?"

She turned and looked at me with desperation in her eyes as I found a spot and parked.

Once we were inside, Lia seemed to calm down some. I knew this was her family's restaurant, so it was no surprise that she knew everyone. People had gathered around to check on her, many already knowing about her broken ankle thanks to the small-town gossip mill. A few people insisted on bringing a chair over for her to sit, but I finally managed to corral everyone over to a table so she could be off her feet.

Ten minutes later, her brother and Kensy walked in. Lia hadn't noticed them at first, which I was unexpectedly happy about because it gave him and me a moment without either of the girls noticing, where we quickly summed each other up without saying a word.

I'd lived in Beaumont Creek long enough to know who Capshaw was and about his playboy lifestyle before he settled down with his little sister's best friend. I hadn't ever had a long conversation with him, but he seemed nice enough. Who knew what he had heard about me? My guess was that it was all negative, and I'd have some reputation rebuilding to do after whatever Lia had told him about Dr. Dickhead.

"Your brother and Kensy are here," I said, bending down so my voice was quiet in her ear.

She looked up and then across the room, where she spotted them headed our way, her brother's eyes narrowed and a scowl on his forehead. I didn't know what Kensy was saying to him through gritted teeth as she forced a smile at us, but it was the way she tried to subtly elbow him in the ribs that got a smile out of me.

As soon as the staff noticed Capshaw, they scurried off, leaving just the four of us at the table.

"Hey, long time no see!" Kensy teased, bending down to hug Lia as Capshaw and I continued to stare at each other.

"I know. I can't get enough of you now that you're back," Lia said, pure happiness in her voice.

Both girls stopped and looked at us, waiting to see what would happen.

"I'm Mason," I said, deciding to take the high road and extended my hand to Capshaw. I wasn't going to win him over by trying to square up against him, so I might as well just put an end to it now.

"I know who you are," he said, his voice still tight but not as tight as his grip on my hand.

Kensy elbowed him again, this time getting him to release me. I pulled back but didn't let on that it had been even slightly uncomfortable. Instead, I squared my shoulders and then looked from him to Kensy.

"Hi, I'm Mason. You must be Kensy. It's so nice to officially meet you." This time, I extended my hand to her, and she took it, her eyes lit up with delight.

"Oh my gosh, I love him for you already," she whispered to Lia, brows furrowed as she stared at my face as if she didn't believe I was real.

"Thank you, I think?" I teased, looking from her to Lia, who had a big smile on her face.

"Relax, Capshaw. We're not going to let this escalate into a pissing contest," Lia said, shifting her focus to her brother. "You're both manly men, now why don't you be a manly man and go order us some food?"

Capshaw shoved his hands into his pockets and glared at his sister before looking at Kensy.

"I thought you said her attitude would be better? It seems like it's only getting worse."

"I don't know, she seems just fine to me," Kensy replied with a giggle. "I like whatever's gotten into her."

"Who," Lia corrected, making the vein in her brother's temple protrude.

"I'm going to go get food," he muttered, then looked at me. "You coming?"

"Um, yeah. Sure. Let me get Lia's order real quick."

"No need. She never changes."

Before I could object, Capshaw walked off to the register. I gave Lia a quizzical look, unsure of what I should do. Sure, her brother likely knew what she usually ordered, but what if she changed her mind and wanted something else? I didn't want to be the dick who fucked up dinner the first time I met her brother and on our first real *date* that didn't involve us eating at home.

She waved me off and nodded for me to join him, so I did.

By the time I reached him, he was already at the register to order.

"Do you know what you want?" he asked, nodding to the menu above the young cashier's head.

"Um, yeah, I'll do the fish and chips. Extra hushpuppies."

I grabbed my wallet and then pulled it away when he shook his head.

"It's my family's restaurant."

"Right," I said, nodding my head. Man, was I already sweating. "Lia mentioned that. But really, I don't mind buying."

"Na, we're good. Thanks, though."

He turned and gave me a tight smile while the cashier put in the order and then gave him a number sign for the table. We walked over to the soda station, where I stood there feeling helpless with two cups in my hand, unsure of what Lia wanted. I started out feeling so confident about this, but now that I had to prove to her brother that I was a good guy for her, I felt clueless about knowing her at all.

"She likes the Diet Coke here. It's the only place she drinks it. For whatever reason, she insists that the carbonation from the drink makes the fish and chips taste that much better."

"Oh, good to know," I said, filling her cup with what I hoped was the right amount of ice before adding the soda. "We haven't eaten here together yet."

"Do you guys go out to eat a lot?" he asked, looking up at me as he placed a lid on the cups he'd already filled.

"No, we've been eating at home a lot since she broke her ankle. I've done the cooking for us, and she seems to be enjoying it."

"Is that why she got a salad for lunch today?"

I couldn't help the laugh that came out.

"I honestly don't know. Lia had mentioned to me that she wanted to eat healthier when she first broke her ankle. She wasn't able to be on her feet to cook, so I took over everything. We've been watching a lot of cooking shows together, and sometimes she'll see stuff that she likes, so I make it for her. I think she just wanted a break from the stuff she used to eat all the time."

Capshaw turned and folded his arms over his chest as he stared at me. My pulse spiked as I watched the judgment on his face, wondering how bad this was going to go.

"You got my sister to watch cooking shows with you *and* to try new foods?"

"Yeah...." I still wasn't sure where this was going.

"Wow. Kensy was right. You have been fixing her attitude."

I turned my head and started coughing, hoping to hide the flush on my cheeks knowing that he wouldn't be so happy about that if he knew how I was *really* fixing her attitude.

Thirty
Lia

Dinner was going even better than I had expected after my brother finally loosened up a bit. It turned out that he and Mason had plenty to talk about once the topic of baseball came up. Kensy and I ignored them and the random stats they were blurting out as we got caught up on all the girly gossip we missed earlier at lunch.

"It's so nice having you back," I said, taking a bite of hushpuppy.

"I'm really happy to be back. California was fun, but I missed home too much. Even with FaceTime, it's not the same as seeing people and getting endless hugs. But you know what I love even more than being home?"

"What's that?"

"Seeing how happy you are with him."

I glanced over at Mason who was still giving my brother his undivided attention as he slipped his hand under the table and grabbed mine.

"Thanks, me too," I said as a yawn started to take over.

"We should get home so you can rest," Mason said, turning his attention to me.

"I'm okay."

"We've gotta go too," Capshaw said. "Mom and Dad have been in heaven babysitting, but Kensy and I want our munchkin back."

"As soon as I'm better, I'll be demanding some munchkin time, too."

"I'll bring her by to see you this week," Kensy said, standing up and grabbing their boxes of food from the table. "Unless you're starting your job this week? I don't remember when you said you were."

"I'm off this week but need to call and check in to make sure it's still okay that I work there, given I can't do the duties I was originally hired for."

"Jane will make stuff work for you; don't worry about it," my brother said, giving me an assuring nod.

"It sucks. I really wanted to jump in and get my feet wet," I said with a sigh.

"Isn't that how you got yourself in this situation to begin with?" Kensy teased, nodding to my cast. "I think you've had enough with wet feet."

"You know what I mean." I laughed. "I really wanted the full experience and to make sure this is what I really want to focus on."

"You can always come back to the ER," Mason added with a wink.

"No way. I'm not working with you again, Dr. Dickhead."

"And why not? We make a great team." He rocked back on his heels, giving me a panty-melting grin.

"Because you make me grumpy when I work for you, and as you've said, no one likes my shitty attitude."

"Lucky for you, I know how to fix that," he whispered, leaning in so only I could hear.

"If he can deal with your shitty attitude, I don't worry about whatever this thing is between you guys," my brother said. "I give a lot of credit to anyone who can take on your multiple personalities. Have you met hangry Lia yet?"

His question wasn't directed at me, even though he was smirking at me when he asked it.

"Ah, yes. I've met hangry Lia. And tired Lia. Cold Lia is alright, but hot Lia is a handful."

"You guys are real funny," I joked sarcastically, bumping shoulders with Capshaw as I pushed past him on my crutches.

We walked out to the parking lot together, and I noticed how my brother hesitated to make sure I was getting in the car okay before he got in and left. It was nice how much he cared about me, even if we tortured each other most of the time.

By the time we got home, I was already tired, but Mason had some new-found energy and decided it was the best time to clean up the house. I tried to help but couldn't keep up. He breezed past me with a laundry basket full of my dirty clothes from Jones's house, which he threw in the washer before hurrying by to unload the dishwasher.

"You're making me dizzy," I teased, grabbing a barstool from under the island and pulling it out. "Did you and my brother do drugs while you were ordering our food? Cause he was way more chill than I expected, and you're going like a mile a minute, doing circles around me."

"No, we didn't do drugs. I just got a burst of energy, so I'm putting it to good use."

"I have something you could do with that energy that would also be putting it to good use," I said, trying my best to sound flirty and not cheesy.

He came around the island holding a bag of trash in his hand.

"Lia, when I'm with you tonight, I want all of my attention to be on you. I don't want to just be burning off energy. You deserve far more than that. Once the chores are done, I'll take a quick shower, and then we'll get to what I really want to do."

"Oh yeah? And what's that?"

"First, I'm going to make love to you."

My eyes widened involuntarily at the word.

"Oh, that's right. The L word gets you all twitchy. Sorry. What I meant to say is that I love you, Lia. As crazy and temperamental as you are, I love every single thing about you."

I opened my mouth and then closed it. The words coming to a mile a minute but resting firmly in the back of my throat where I couldn't speak them.

"Mason," I said softly instead.

"I'm not going to take them back or apologize for saying it. That's how I feel. You might not love me yet, but you will. For now, you can process the fact that I love you, and I don't plan to stop anytime soon."

"Have I ever told you that you're the king of romance?" I teased, nodding to the bag of trash he was still holding.

"Trust me, I know plenty about romance. Could I have picked a better, more *romantic* way to tell you how I feel? Probably. But if I told you while I was balls deep inside you, there would be the opportunity for you to doubt whether I meant it or if I was just lost in the moment. The fact that I decided to confess how I feel while doing something as mundane and boring as taking out the trash should assure you that my feelings are solid and real. Nothing is going to change them, no matter how good or how bad the situation is at the moment when I say it."

My heart fluttered wildly in my chest as a warmth spread through me from his words.

"I love you too, Mason."

I reached up and pulled him down to me as my lips eagerly found his.

Thirty- One

Mason

I told Lia I loved her while holding a bag of trash in my hand.

I was a fucking idiot.

Lia deserved so much more than that, and while, at the time, it made sense in my head, I hadn't been able to stop regretting *how* I told her. The first time should have been special, but I was so obsessed with making sure she knew how I really felt that the words just burst out of me.

I also might have still been riding the adrenaline high from having dinner with her brother. While I didn't usually care what people thought of me, I couldn't help but want to impress him. Maybe it was because he was around my age and I wanted him to know that I wasn't just dicking around with his sister, or maybe it was because I genuinely cared what he thought. Either way, I was feeling out of sorts and off my game tonight.

But even with the lackluster way I'd told her I loved her, Lia said it back. And I believed her. Which was wild because it wasn't that long ago that she was plotting my murder and telling me how much she hated me. Now, she was curled up beside me in my bed, fast asleep as I lay awake, contemplating how we got here.

I wasn't the kind of guy to fall in love and settle down with a woman, so this felt completely brand new to me. But in the best way. After things happened with Jess, I shut myself off from people and kept my head down while I worked through med school. I hadn't allowed myself to get involved with anyone because I didn't want to allow anyone to risk jeopardizing everything I had worked so hard for. But with Lia, she didn't feel like someone I had to worry about that with.

Lia shifted and groaned next to me as she tried to get comfortable, so I let go of her so she could sleep. It was hotter than usual, and even though she was following the rules of sleeping naked in my bed, that didn't mean we weren't getting hot and sticky. I gently climbed out of bed once I heard her snoring again and headed to the kitchen for a drink of water.

I had one last day home with Lia before I had to return to work, and I hated the thought of leaving her. While it'd been my idea all along to be here to take care of her, I hadn't considered how much I'd grow attached to her or how much I would miss her. The simple things that others would consider boring—like binge-watching cooking shows together, were what I looked forward to.

I sat on the couch and flipped through channels on the TV, praying that I would soon get tired enough to head back to bed. But I was restless and knew myself well enough to know that wasn't likely going to happen tonight.

The ice water was refreshing, helping me to cool off from the heat. I felt guilty for watching any of the shows Lia and I usually watched together without her, so I changed it to some infomercial and closed my eyes. Soon, my body relaxed against the couch, and my mind began to quiet down.

I hadn't planned on sleeping on the couch, but when I smelled coffee brewing, my eyes flew open, and I looked around frantically to find Lia making herself at home in my kitchen. I got up and rushed over to where she was attempting to cook breakfast, my thoughts racing as I tried to calculate every risk with what she was doing.

"Relax," she said with a soft laugh. "I have to be able to cook for myself while you're at work, so why not start now?"

"You should have woken me up so I could help," I replied, noticing the bacon she had already started and the pan of frozen hashbrowns on the back skillet.

"You seemed like you needed the rest." She looked up at me for a second, her eyes scanning my face as she looked for something. "You didn't sleep in the bed last night."

I shook my head and gently rubbed my hand along her back.

"I was super restless and didn't want to wake you. I came to get a glass of water and thought watching TV for a bit might help. I didn't mean to fall asleep out here."

"Oh. I just thought maybe you regretted telling me you loved me last night and needed some space."

She cracked an egg and dropped it into the skillet as if she hadn't just said that.

"Hey," I said, grabbing her elbow and turning her to face me once I knew she wasn't going to burn herself. "Why would you think that?"

She shrugged and refused to look at me.

"Lia…"

"I don't know. No one has ever said they loved me before, so I wouldn't be surprised if you suddenly changed your mind."

My eyebrows raised high on my forehead.

"Lia, I wouldn't have said it if I didn't mean it. I know that things are moving quickly, and I'm sorry if that scares you. But if there's anything you can trust, it's how much you mean to me and that I will do anything in the world for you."

"Anything?" she asked, batting her eyes at me.

I nodded.

"Just name it."

"Would you finish making breakfast? My foot is starting to hurt, and I might have bitten off more than I could chew with this whole *independence* thing."

"Of course. Go sit down, and I'll bring you your coffee. How do you want your eggs?"

"Scrambled with cheese, please."

"You got it."

I handed her the crutches and made sure she was good to go before I turned my attention back to breakfast.

"What do you want to watch this morning?" Lia asked from the couch, making my heart swarm with happiness with how comfortable she seemed here already. We hadn't discussed actually living together, but was there really a big difference between her staying with Jones temporarily or staying with me for the foreseeable future? Not in my opinion.

"We can start the final season of Champion Chef if you want," I offered, flipping the eggs in the skillet. I knew that Lia had started my food first, which added more of those warm fuzzy feelings I was starting to get used to.

"Do you think we can finish the whole season today?"

"If we don't do anything else but sit on the couch and binge all day, yeah, we should be able to."

"Do you want to?"

There was excitement in her voice that I loved as I handed her her favorite mug filled with espresso blend coffee and hazelnut creamer—two things I never used to have in my house until Lia.

"I would love to." I kissed the top of her head and then returned to the kitchen to finish our food. This was the life I never knew I needed, and now that I had it, I couldn't imagine anything different.

Thirty-Two
Lia

Mondays sucked. But today was especially sucky because it was Mason's first day back to work, and I was bored out of my mind alone in his house. I considered going back to Jones's place to see if I felt less restless there but then decided not to. While I had gotten better about getting around on my crutches, I didn't want to risk doing too much too soon and not having anyone around if I needed help. The last thing I wanted was for Mason to feel like he had to take more time off from work to take care of me— even if I wouldn't mind the company.

But the fact of the matter was that we hadn't been living in the real world these past two weeks. Mason had been considerate to take off to help me while Bella and Jones were out of town, but that was over now. He had a job and other responsibilities, and I was going to be starting my new job with Jane soon. I was initially supposed to start today, but there was a hiccup in the schedule this week, and they asked me to start next week instead.

Mason and I had talked several times over the past few days about what the plan would be moving forward with Jones and Bella coming back this weekend from their honeymoon. He offered to help me move my stuff from their house to his, but for some reason, I was reluctant to. I was comfortable at his house, but something kept nagging at me, telling me not to rush things.

I tried to chalk it up to being nervous about being in a committed, serious relationship, but it felt like more than that, and I hated it. It was like I was constantly waiting for the other shoe to drop and some bomb to come falling in my lap, ruining everything I had come to love.

I went to the fridge and grabbed a yogurt, thankful that Mason had taken the time to do grocery shopping yesterday so I would have quick and easy meal options this week while he was gone. He wouldn't be home until late tonight, but had already put dinner in the crock pot before he left so I wouldn't have to worry about trying to cook. Even though two weeks had passed since I broke my ankle, I still couldn't stand to be on it for long periods of time.

There was nothing on TV as I sat on the couch and ate my yogurt, wondering how I was going to entertain myself while he was gone all day. As if the universe could sense my disdain, my phone started ringing on the coffee table. I reached for it, smiling when I saw Kensy's name on the screen.

"How did you know I was going out of my mind?" I asked as a way of greeting.

"Because I know you too well. Brayleigh and I are going out to run some errands, and I thought maybe we could stop by when we're done. Maybe bring you a latte and a scone from Rockin' Rooster?"

"You had me at latte."

Kensy laughed, the phone making noise as she attempted to do something in the background.

"I knew I would. However, I thought it would be the whole—*I'm bringing your niece to see you* part that would get you. But it's alright; I won't tell your brother that you chose coffee over your own flesh and blood."

"You know I love to see her."

"But not as much as you love the buttery, flaky scones and hazelnut lattes from Rockin' Rooster," she retorted with a chuckle.

"There's nothing I love more than those."

"Not even Mason?"

Fire shot through my veins as heat rushed through me, guilt immediately taking over as I considered how true those words might be.

"I'll see you in an hour," she said, letting me off the hook.

"Alright, see you soon."

I hung up the phone and took a bite of my yogurt, contemplating what I had just said.

An hour and a half later, Kensy showed up with her arms full and my cutie patootie niece sitting on her hip.

"She had a meltdown at Rockin' Rooster, so Abby had to help me. Apparently, the only way to calm her down was with cake. Do NOT tell your brother that."

I pressed my lips together to keep from laughing and pretended to zip them shut.

"Your latte probably isn't as hot as you'd like it, but I can microwave it if you want. Sorry, I tried to get here as quickly as possible, but things never go as planned anymore."

"You're fine. Thank you for getting me coffee; I appreciate it."

I waited for Kensy to get herself settled, then led her and Brayleigh over to the couch. I grabbed the remote and looked for a kid show on Netflix while Kensy set her down on a blanket on the floor with a few toys she pulled out of the diaper bag.

"So, how are things going here?" Kensy said, looking around the space for the first time and taking a drink of her iced coffee.

"Good," I replied, letting out a sigh that was too heavy to avoid being noticed by Kensy.

"But?"

"But what?" I looked away, pretending to focus on my niece instead of avoiding my best friend.

"There's a but. I can hear it."

My eyes looked up and found hers.

"I don't know. I have no idea what it is, but it just feels like things are too good to be true."

"What makes you say that?"

"Nothing. Everything." I tipped my head back and shut my eyes as I shook my head. "I just don't know what it is, but something feels off. I feel restless and uncomfortable, and I can't put my finger on what it is. Mason offered to help me move my stuff over from Jones's house, but I keep putting it off. Like, I don't even live there, yet I can't leave a temporary home to stay with the guy who I said I love you to? Like, what is that?"

Kensy's face softened as she listened, her eyes calm and caring.

"Do you love him?" she asked softly. "Because it's okay if you're not sure. Things happened really quickly between you guys, and you went from hating him to falling so quickly for him."

"Whose side are you on here?" I asked, a little too defensively. "Weren't you the one just telling me a week or so ago that you thought I was in love with him, and now you're questioning it?"

"I'm just saying that maybe things changed. I'm not trying to disregard anything, Lia. I'm just trying to help you work through whatever is bothering you. Even if *I* thought you were in love, that doesn't mean that it's what you're feeling, and that's okay. You don't have to be in love. You can be headed that way but not quite there, and no one would fault you for it."

"Mason probably would," I said with a strained laugh. "He would probably send me in to get my head evaluated for being the crazy girl who didn't know how to be in a committed relationship and who says stuff she doesn't mean."

"How can you possibly know what it means to be in love? Lia, you might have dated lots of guys before. And I mean *lots*—"

"Gee, thanks."

"BUT you've never been in love with any of them."

I eyed her warily, unsure of whether I was still mad at her or if she was starting to make actual sense.

"You've been with Mason for a little over two weeks," Kensy said, shifting on the couch to face me directly as Brayleigh played. "You went from hating the guy to having to rely on him to help you when you broke your ankle. You were forced to let your guard down with him, and when you did, you saw a different side of him. Being stuck together for that long allowed you both to get to know each other outside of work, and I think you really like who he is now that you know him. But Lia, this all happened so fast for you guys that I'm not surprised that you're overthinking everything and feeling worried that something bad is going to happen. When was the last time something good happened with a guy you were dating?"

"Never."

"Exactly. But just because you're used to something bad happening doesn't mean that's what is going to happen with Mason. I know that you're scared to allow yourself to jump in with both feet, but sometimes that's how the best things in life happen."

"Yeah, and I only have one good foot. It's even more risky for me," I joked, loving the way her lips curled into a smile.

"You know what I mean. Just give it some time. It's not like he asked you to marry him. He just asked to move your stuff over to the house you're already technically living in. Besides, if anything happens and this doesn't work out, it's not like it's that hard to move stuff back over to Jones and Bella's place. It's not like they're going to change the locks and kick you out the second your stuff is gone."

"You never know. You didn't see the way they were constantly looking at each other when I was there—like they could just rip each other's clothes off and go at it if I wasn't in the room. I think they'll definitely reconsider having a roommate once they know I have somewhere else I can go. It was different when everyone thought I was going to end up homeless and on the streets."

"You were never going to be homeless," Kensy said with a laugh. "You know that your brother and I would have taken you in as well."

"Oh, please," I snorted. "You guys are worse than Bella and Jones. I know what happens to all the extra guacamole you guys take home from Tipsy Taquito—no thanks."

Kensy blushed redder than I'd ever seen before, and I wondered if someday I would be that affected by Mason when someone talked about how intense our chemistry was.

Thirty-Three
Mason

When I got home, I was pleasantly surprised to find Lia at the table with two plates of food set out for us and a bottle of wine. She looked beautiful with no makeup on and her hair tossed loosely on her head. It felt like it had been forever since I'd last seen her, even though it was barely over ten hours.

"Hey, look at you," I said, smiling and kissing the top of her head before setting my stuff down on the counter. "Thank you for getting dinner ready."

"You did all the hard work," she replied with a soft laugh. "I just took it out of the crockpot and tried to control myself from diving in before you got here. It's smelled amazing all day."

"You didn't have to wait for me, silly girl. You should have eaten if you were hungry."

"I know, but I wanted to. I thought it would be nice to sit down and have dinner together."

I smiled, loving how she wanted to spend time with me. It wasn't just me being completely and utterly infatuated with her; it was reciprocal.

"Absolutely. Let me go wash up, and then we can get started."

I went to the sink, washed my hands, and then grabbed a few bottles of water from the fridge before sitting down with Lia at the table. She poured each of us a glass of wine and then smiled as she lifted hers and took a sip.

"How was work?" she asked, cutting into the piece of roast on her plate and bringing her attention back to me.

"It was good. Nothing too exciting, which is always nice when I'm tired. But I did miss being home and binge-watching TV with you. How was your day?"

"It was good. I was feeling a little restless, but then Kensy came over and brought Brayleigh to see me. It was nice having company for a while. I thought for sure I would love my down time alone in the house, but it turns out I'm pretty boring and need others to keep me entertained."

She laughed and shrugged.

"You're not boring at all. I'm glad you had some time with them, baby. That's really awesome."

"Thanks. It still feels kinda weird to invite people over to your house, and I know I should have asked first—"

"*Our* house," I corrected, hating that she still didn't consider this her home. "I know it's all new, and it will take a while for you to adjust to everything, but this is your house, too, Lia. You don't have to ask before inviting anyone over, and you don't have to check with me if you want to do something. Please don't stress over stuff like that."

"I'm trying." She sighed heavily and stabbed at her potato with her fork. "I don't know why it's so hard for me just to let go."

She shook her head, and I could see the thoughts racing through it, along with the things she wasn't ready to say.

"Lia, don't put all of this pressure on yourself. Trust me, there's no need to worry about these little things. Let's just take things one day at a time. You're going to make yourself sick worrying about things that don't really matter in the long run."

Her face softened as if my words had calmed the storm that was raging inside.

I shifted gears and went into a story about the old man who came in today with a fishing lure stuck in his neck. It was one of the gnarliest fishing injuries I had seen, but the worst part was that his wife had brought him in, and she couldn't stop laughing. It wasn't that she had found it funny; it was a nervous reaction, and every time she got the giggles, he would start laughing, making it harder to remove. They had been married for over forty years, and he knew this was how she reacted during stressful times, so he didn't mind the constant laughing. By the time I was done removing the lure, I had found myself with new-found relationship goals.

Once dinner was done, I shredded the rest of the meat and chopped up the potatoes to make burritos for tomorrow night. I wanted to keep things as simple as possible for Lia while I was gone, which meant having meals prepped and ready to go. She had already retreated to the bedroom while I finished up, and I prayed she wasn't already in bed. I had missed her all day and wanted just a little more time with her tonight before I had to give her up so she could rest.

When I walked into the bedroom, I was pleasantly surprised to find her naked and sprawled out across the bed.

"You didn't make dessert, so I thought I would improvise," she said, chewing her lower lip.

"This is better than anything I could have made," I replied, pulling my shirt over my head and tossing it behind me. My cock was already hardening at the sight of her pebbled nipples from the air conditioning and the slickness glistening between her thighs. I shrugged off the rest of my clothes and climbed onto the bed, immediately lowering myself between her thighs.

Her fingers dug into my hair, pulling tightly as I slid my tongue through her folds and then flicked her clit. It had only been a day since I went down on her, but it still felt like too long. Wayyyy too long. I could live between Lia's thighs, eating her all day, every day.

She moaned and arched her back, her body already as used to my touch as I was used to reading it to know when she was getting close. I loved that I could bring this side out of her so easily, arousing her quickly with soft touches and building the pressure and intensity as she needed.

I inserted two fingers and fucked her with them while I continued to devour her pussy with my mouth. Within seconds, I felt the first few spasms against my lips as she came undone and let her orgasm crash over her.

"That was amazing," she whispered as I kissed my way up her body and lined my cock up at her entrance.

"You're amazing."

Her eyes fluttered open, the beautiful blue reminding me of happy, sunny days.

"Don't make me wait, Mason. Give me that cock."

"Such a dirty mouth," I teased, lowering my mouth over hers.

Then I slid inside, holding her tight as her pussy wrapped around me, fitting like a glove. I lifted her legs, allowing myself to push in deeper as she rocked against me, already eager for the hard thrusts she loved.

Things with Lia weren't always easy, but making love to her was the one thing that always came naturally to me.

Thirty-Four
Lia

The first few days Mason was back at work were hard to get used to, but by Thursday, I finally felt a little more comfortable being home by myself in his house. Which was funny because just as I got used to it, it would all change again in a few days. He was off tomorrow, and then next week, I would start my new job with Jane, so I wouldn't be home anyway.

He had made sure to put dinner in the crockpot before he left this morning, but the savory aroma of lasagna floating in the air was making my stomach growl nonstop. I had been a mindless, bottomless pit this morning, eating anything and everything in sight, yet nothing could cure the craving I had for the lasagna.

By two o'clock, I was feeling restless again and decided to do some tidying up. Mason's house was always clean, but there were a few things that I knew needed to be taken care of that he hadn't gotten a chance to do yet. I hobbled to the utility closet and grabbed some cleaning supplies, knowing I could at least clean the sink and wipe down the counters.

There wasn't much clutter in his house, something I had noticed early on. He kept things simple and clean, which was different than how I usually kept things. I sprayed some cleaner onto the cloth I had seen him use before and started on the counter by the fridge.

Mason's iPad was charging, so I picked it up so I could clean underneath it. I hadn't realized that it was turned on until the screen lit up and a new email message appeared on it. I knew that it wasn't any of my business and that I should have just set it down and let it be, but when I saw the subject of the email, my curiosity was piqued.

Against my better judgment, I unlocked the screen and opened the message.

Subject: Second Interview

From: Charles St. Luke

To: Mason Dickson

Date: June 4, 2024 2:17

Dr. Dickson,

I apologize for the delay in touching base with you after your first interview with our practice, however, we had some unforeseen changes within our department that required our immediate attention. We are still very interested in meeting with you again to continue the interview process and discuss your application for the position of attending physician.

I remember you mentioned that you had a change to your availability as you were caring for a family member who had suffered an injury. If you can please let me know your current availability, we can move forward with setting up your second interview.

We understand that making travel arrangements to do an in-person interview in San Diego will take some time. Please let us know how we can assist you with this if you're still interested in interviewing for this position.

Regards,

Charles St. Luke

Director of Human Resources

My heart stopped beating for a split second as I read the email a second time. Mason was looking for another job, and he hadn't even bothered to tell me about it. And it had been recently because they knew that he was taking time off to take care of me.

I quickly exited the message, making sure to mark it as unread before turning off the iPad and setting it back on the counter. My thoughts were racing as I tried to figure out what all of this meant.

Why was Mason looking for another job? Were there others he had applied for? Was he planning to move regardless? How long had he been considering leaving? But more importantly—why would he lead me on and tell me he loved me when he knew he was just going to turn around and leave? That was the part that left a burning hole in my stomach.

Thirty-Five
Mason

The day was dragging, and I couldn't wait to get off and head home to see Lia. I was off tomorrow and already planned to sit around and watch TV with her, just like we had done the last few weeks before the real world snuck up on us. Typically, I was a relatively active person and preferred to spend time outside of the house, hiking or going for a run, but being forced to stay inside to take care of Lia had brought out a different side I didn't know I had. Relaxing with a beautiful woman on the couch wasn't a bad way to spend the days.

By four o'clock, the ER had slowed down, and I finally got a chance to sit down and take a quick break. I opened a protein bar and shoved it into my mouth, hungry from working through the day without lunch. I opened my phone to see if there were any missed messages from Lia—not that I expected there to be any, given I hadn't heard it or felt it buzz all day, but my heart hoped nonetheless.

There were a few spam emails that I deleted and then one that made my fingers stop before opening it.

It was an email I would have been jumping up and down over a few weeks ago, but now it made my stomach churn seeing it.

When I first submitted my application to Valley Peak Medical, I didn't expect much. I was feeling bored and needed something different, so I figured why not apply? A change of scenery might be exactly what I needed. Going from a steady-paced ER in a small town to a Level 1 trauma center in the city would be challenging, and I had been looking forward to it.

I opened the email and scanned over it a few times, not making any effort to respond. If things were different and I didn't have Lia at home waiting for me, I would be booking a flight and getting the hell out of Beaumont Creek in a heartbeat. But knowing that she was at my house, waiting for me to come home and have dinner with her, was what stopped me in my tracks.

Things had changed so quickly in a few weeks that I couldn't even keep up with everything and how my feelings had shifted so drastically. But maybe that was what it was like to be in love. Giving up the things you *thought* you wanted in order to have the person you *knew* you wanted. But the problem was that Lia and love were never supposed to be on my radar. I wasn't supposed to find someone who would challenge everything I thought I wanted in my life and make me second guess what I was really working toward.

For so long, I knew I wanted to put my everything into my career. I wanted to save lives and give back to my community. I wanted to practice medicine and solve the mysteries no one else could diagnose. I wanted to have a purpose. I wanted to be needed.

But there was something I wanted even more than that, and that was Lia.

I put my phone away, tossed my wrapper in the trash, and got back to work. The sooner the day here was done, the sooner I could go home and be with the only person in the world whom I cared about right now.

<u>Thirty- Six</u>
Lia

"Are you sure this is okay?" I asked, frowning as Bella moved around the living room, moving their luggage out of the way.

"Of course it is. Why wouldn't it be?" She planted her hands on her hips and looked around.

"Because I was supposed to be moved out and living with Mason before you guys got back. Now I'm back to crashing at your house, and you're fresh off your honeymoon. You guys probably hate not having alone time in your own house again."

"Stop it." She reached out and grabbed my shoulders, forcing me to look at her. "I don't know what happened or why the sudden change of plans, but that doesn't matter, Lia. If you need a place to stay, you have a place to stay. No questions asked and no deadlines for when you need to leave. Got it?"

I nodded, chewing the inside of my cheek to keep from crying.

After reading the email on Mason's iPad, I finished cleaning up and then grabbed my stuff, and got out of there before he got home. I felt bad for leaving, especially since I didn't bother to text or call him—I just left him a note on a sticky pad that said I needed time and to leave me alone. It was really immature, but I didn't know what else to do. I freaked out and ran because it was what I did best.

Plus, if he didn't have the courage to tell me he was looking for a new job—out of state, no less—why would I expect him to sit down and have an honest conversation with me about our future? He clearly knew he wasn't planning to stay, yet he allowed me to let my guard down and fall for him and his stupid magical mouth that brought me the best orgasms I'd ever had.

"Do I need to go kick his ass?" Jones asked, coming in from bringing the rest of their stuff in from the car.

"No," I said with a soft laugh and shake of my head. "But thank you."

"Alright. If you change your mind, just let me know."

"Thanks."

"I'm going to help Lia get situated, then we can go out to dinner," Bella offered.

"I would offer to cook, but…" Jones smiled awkwardly, making all of us laugh since we knew the chance of him burning it would be high.

"I appreciate the offer, baby, but maybe we go a few days before we try to set anything on fire? We just got home. Let's enjoy being smoke-free for a bit." Bella patted his arm gently.

"Deal."

I laughed as they kissed, clearly stopping themselves from getting carried away when they remembered they had an audience.

I felt bad for intruding on their space, so I went to my room and closed the door. It wasn't like this was any better for trying to get Mason off my mind when I remembered all of the dirty stuff we'd done together in here. Unless I gave in and went to stay with my brother and Kensy for a while, I was doomed to be stuck somewhere that reminded me of Dr. Dickhead.

I sat down on the bed and felt my phone vibrate in my pocket. I knew it was Mason because it was easily the seventh time it had gone off in the last ten minutes, which was around the time he got home and would have found my note.

I pulled it out and unlocked the screen, finding several messages from him.

Mason: Hey, what's going on? Are you okay?

Mason: Lia, I got your note, and I'm worried. What happened?

Mason: Please let me know you're okay. I'm trying my best to give you space like you asked, but the only thing that is stopping me from barging over there is that Jones just threatened to come cook something in my house, and I don't need it to catch on fire.

Mason: Whatever I did, I'm sorry. Please just talk to me.

Mason: The door is unlocked whenever you want to come back home.

Mason: This is still your home, Lia.

Mason: I love you.

The last message broke me, shattering my heart as tears streamed down my face. How could he do what he did and then still have the nerve to tell me he loved me? Did he not understand the impact his decision would have on me when he decided to up and leave for California? Did he expect that I would just give up everything here and go with him, or was he genuinely okay with walking away from whatever this thing was between us so he could chase his dreams?

Me: Please don't say that. You don't know what love is if you think this is it.

Me: I knew better than to stop hating you, Dr. Dickhead.

Thirty- Seven
Mason

"I knew better than to stop hating you, Dr. Dickhead."

Ouch. I couldn't say that didn't hurt. But I had no idea what had set Lia off and spooked her so bad that she just left without saying a word. Something had happened, but I was completely clueless.

It wasn't like I wasn't used to her being hot-headed and temperamental, but this was different. She acted like she was hurt by something I did, but I had no clue what. I had simply gone to work and then came home to an empty house and a note that said she needed space.

I was tempted to ask Jones if he knew what was going on, but he didn't seem that happy to see me, so I decided it was best just to let things go until Lia calmed down enough for me to talk to her. I didn't know how long that would be given that I didn't even know what I did wrong.

I spent Friday at home by myself, deep cleaning to keep myself busy so I wouldn't head next door to try to talk to her. I knew she wasn't going to give in until she was ready, so I just had to wait it out.

In the meantime, I responded to the email for the second interview and declined. Even if things didn't work out between me and Lia, I couldn't see myself moving to

California right now. Not if there was a chance that things could work later for me and Lia. I wasn't willing to jeopardize having a shot at this by taking the interview and considering moving my life. Now was not the time for rash decisions, and I knew that. As hard as it was, I just had to wait this out and hope for the best.

Thirty-Eight
Lia

My first day at my new job with Jane went better than I had expected. Probably because I assumed the whole day would be a mess after showing up and finding a dozen roses waiting for me with a sweet note from Mason wishing me good luck. Not only that, he also had a knee scooter delivered so I could get around easily. I had burst into random tears, confusing and startling most of the staff before I was whisked away by Jane and shown around.

It wasn't as busy as I imagined it would be, and I was thankful to have plenty of time to get used to things. Jane had gone out of her way to make as many arrangements for me as possible so I could get the hands-on experience I wanted without being limited by my broken ankle. I immediately felt like part of the team, and even though it hadn't been a full day, I knew this was what I wanted to do with my life. I wanted to work with kids and feel the joy that came about every time I interacted with them.

Bella and Kensy had insisted on taking me out for dinner to celebrate my first day, so we headed to Tipsy Taquito for drinks and tacos. I was tired and just wanted to go home, but I didn't want to tell them that and ruin the celebration they had planned.

When we got there, my brother and Jones were already there, holding a table for us in the back. It wasn't a surprise that they had already ordered for us as well, so my food and an icy-cold margarita were already waiting for me.

I sat down and leaned my crutches against the wall behind me, feeling a stab of disappointment that Mason wasn't there. I knew I had to move on and not allow myself to continue to dwell on things between us, but it was hard to just tell myself it was over and hope that I could fall out of love quicker than I had fallen into it.

"To Lia," Kensy said, lifting her glass in the air.

I lifted mine and clinked it against the others, smiling to show my appreciation for all of them being there. I felt terrible that they all likely knew it was forced, but I couldn't help the way I felt.

Thankfully, everyone started talking, and the conversation moved to Bella and Jones's honeymoon, taking the attention off me. I took a bite of taco and chewed, not even tasting any of the flavors I usually did with them. It was disappointing, but everything in my life was that way right now because of stupid Dr. Dickhead.

I had my head down, focused on getting the food into my mouth so I could say I ate dinner when I felt Kensy nudge my side with her elbow. I scooted over the best I could and kept eating, assuming I had somehow encroached on her space.

"He's here," she said tightly through her teeth, trying not to get anyone else's attention.

"Who is?"

It was dumb to ask because literally everyone I knew was sitting at the table with us. Not only that, but the tingles that spread over me from knowing he was there was a dead giveaway. I felt his eyes on me as my skin flushed with heat from the intense look he was giving me from across the room. My fork fell from my fingers, clanging against the plate and startling everyone else.

My brother was the first to turn to see who I was looking at, his neck tightening as he gripped the table and tried to stand up.

"Sit down," Kensy demanded, pulling his attention back to her. He looked from her to me, waiting for me to give him the go-ahead to talk to Mason. Or kick his ass—who knew what my brother was thinking as the vein in his forehead continued to protrude.

As if sensing the hostility coming from our table, Mason bravely made his way over, ignoring the looks from everyone else as he kept his focus on me.

"Can we please talk for a minute?" he asked, squatting down beside me.

"Talk about what? Your new life in California? Na, I think I'm good. Best of luck to you, though, Dr. Dickhead."

My jaw clenched as I tried to keep my anger at the surface so I didn't give in when Mason's fingers lightly brushed against my thigh. I needed to stay angry because I couldn't trust myself not to forget everything that happened and get ambushed again when he decided to leave for good.

His head pulled back in surprise as he processed my words.

"Wait. What?" He shook his head and frowned. "What are you talking about?"

"You know damn well what I'm talking about."

"I don't think I do. I don't have a new life in California."

"You sure about that?" I asked, cocking my head to the side as venom wrapped around my words. "Because I know all about your job offer in San Diego. I saw the email come through on your iPad while I was cleaning, and yes, I know I shouldn't have read it, but I did. And it's a good thing I did since you apparently had no intentions of telling me about it."

He stood up and scrubbed a hand down his face before tipping his head back.

"You've got to be kidding me," he grunted loud enough for everyone at the table to hear. "That's what this has been all about?"

"Seriously?" I asked, standing up and reaching for my crutches. If we were going to do this, we were going to do it face to face, and he would have to look me in the eye. "I tell you that I know about your plans to move to California and you're acting like it's no big deal?"

"Yeah, because it's not."

I pulled back, narrowing my eyes at him. He had some fucking nerve.

"You're kidding me, right? Because if not, then you truly are such a dick."

"You don't even know what you're talking about, Lia. You took something you didn't know anything about and made a mountain out of a molehill."

"Well, maybe I would know more if you actually took the time to tell me about it! Don't you think I deserve to know that the guy I'm falling in love with is planning to up and move to California? Spoiler alert, but that's a pretty huge deal, dumbass."

"Of course it is. But I wasn't planning to go, Lia. I took the initial interview *long before* you broke your ankle. They had reached out to do a second interview when you got hurt, and I asked them to postpone it. As you saw in the email, they had some unexpected things happen on their end, which delayed them reaching out again. Honestly, I forgot all about the job until that email came in the other day. I didn't tell you about it because there was nothing to tell."

"Yes there was!" I shouted, cringing when I felt more eyes on us. We were causing a scene, but I couldn't get myself to back down. I had words to say, and I wasn't going to be silenced.

"How so?"

"Because Mason! You were planning a different life and didn't even bother to tell me. How is that even fair? How do you expect me to trust that something like this won't happen in the future? You want me to plant roots and move in with you, but you've already got one foot out the door!"

"None of that matters because I don't want anything unless it involves you, Lia! Even if I had the second interview with them and they offered me the job, I wouldn't have taken it unless you had come to me and told me you wanted to move to California. Then I would do it for *you*. This isn't about just me anymore—that's what you don't get. Your happiness is all that I want, and I'll do whatever it takes to make sure you're always happy, Lia. You should know that by now. I've shown you repeatedly that there's not a damn thing I won't do for you."

"But you considered moving, Mason—that's a huge thing!"

"BEFORE. I. FUCKING. FELL. IN. LOVE. WITH. YOU."

My eyes widened with how angry he was getting, and I couldn't lie—it was a fucking turn-on.

"You are the *most infuriating, stubborn* person I have ever met," he growled, shaking his head.

"True story," my brother chimed in, earning a glare from me but a faint smile from Mason.

"What? She is." He shrugged and lifted his hands as Kensy kicked him under the table.

"Lia, I can't tell you how much you've changed my life in the few weeks we were together. I never would have imagined that I would fall in love that quickly, but I did. And I haven't stopped loving you since. Even when you got mad and ran away instead of talking to me."

"I was upset," I said, defending myself.

"Yeah, and I'm your boyfriend. If this relationship is ever going to work, you have to talk to me when things are bothering you. Don't you see how much stress and heartache we could have saved ourselves if you would have just asked me about the email when you first saw it?"

My cheeks flamed with embarrassment because he was right. So much time and energy could have been used on better stuff had I just talked to him about it when I first saw it. But I was scared and had been waiting for the other shoe to drop for so long that it felt like this was it.

"I'm sorry," I said softly, not looking up to meet his eyes.

"What was that?" he asked, stepping in to wrap his arms around me.

"I said, *I'm sorry*," I repeated, this time my teeth clenched together.

"I still couldn't hear it."

"I said I'm sorry," I yelled loudly, this time grabbing everyone's attention in the restaurant.

Mason's smile spread from ear to ear as he pulled me against his chest and lowered his mouth to mine.

"I'm sorry, too. I should have told you about the job, but honestly, it never crossed my mind. I was so happy with how things were going between us that I didn't give it a second thought and had forgotten about it. I never meant to hurt you, Lia."

"And I'm sorry that I didn't just come out and ask you about it. I should have given you a chance to explain what was going on."

"Hey, Jones, go to the kitchen and try to cook something," my brother said, nodding to his friend.

"Why?" Jones asked, his brows furrowed in confusion.

"Because I think the universe is out of whack. My sister just admitted she was wrong and actually said *I'm sorry* to someone. If you can cook something without starting a fire, I'll know for sure we're officially in the Twilight Zone."

"Shut up," I hissed, swatting the back of his head. "I say sorry when I mean it."

"You've never said it to me," my brother countered.

"Because I've never meant it with you."

I stuck my tongue out, ready to go head-to-head with my brother, until Mason nuzzled his mouth against my neck and pressed a light kiss.

"Why don't you finish your dinner, then we can go home, and I'll fix your attitude for you," he offered quietly, spreading fire through my veins.

Thirty-Nine

Mason

"Do you need anything else?" I asked, handing Lia her ice water while she got situated on the couch. She had only been gone for four days, but that was far too long for me.

We had gotten home from Tipsy Taquito an hour ago after I was forced to stay and join them for dinner after impressing her brother by standing up to his sister. I was worried that he would be upset with me being so forward with her, but he bought me a shot instead and told me I was the *Lia Whisperer*.

It felt nice knowing that the air had been cleared between us and I hated that things even got to that point, all because of a simple misunderstanding. If I had known that Lia had seen the email, I would have made sure to talk to her about it right away so there was no room for her to have to guess what my true intentions were. But none of that mattered now, and I was ready to move forward.

"I'm good, but thank you."

I sat down beside her and pulled her into my arms, never wanting to be away from her again.

"I have a question for you, though," she said, leaning her head up to look at me.

"Sure, what is it?"

"If you and I hadn't ever gotten together, would you consider taking that job in California?"

I thought about it for a second before answering.

"Probably."

Her body stiffened beneath me as she reacted to the answer she probably didn't want to hear.

"But only because I was unhappy and looking for something different in life."

"Are you happy now?"

"The happiest I've ever been."

She relaxed against me, seeming content with my answer.

"Are you happy?" I asked, figuring now was the time to have the conversation about what we wanted out of life.

"I am. I like it here in Beaumont Creek and love being close to my family. Working with Jane today was everything I had hoped it would be, and I'm super excited to see how things go there over the summer. I can't think of anything else I could want that I don't already have."

I linked my fingers through hers and snuggled her tighter against my body.

"Well, there might be *one thing* I want that I don't have," she added.

"Oh yeah? What's that, baby?"

"I want my ankle to be better already so I can ride your cock the way I want to. I want you to fuck me in ways we haven't been able to because of the stupid cast."

"Soon enough, baby. Soon enough."

"I also want a puppy," she added with a laugh. "It's such a random thing, I know. I've always wanted one, but my parents always said no. I don't know why, but having a dog of my own makes it feel like it would be the next step in being an actual adult. Like being able to prove to everyone that I can keep something other than myself alive. But then again, maybe I should start with something simpler, like a plant. That would probably be the bigger test since I tend to kill everything I touch."

"Well, pet ownership is a big responsibility, so I could see how that would make you feel like an adult. And plants can be super temperamental, so don't be too hard on yourself."

"Someone used to say *I* was temperamental. Are you now comparing me to a plant?"

"Yes. Like a venus fly trap, to be specific."

She laughed as she nudged me in the side with her elbow.

"What kind of dog would you get?" I asked, gently brushing my fingers down her arm. Hearing Lia talk about something she wanted did something to me, and I couldn't stop wanting to know everything about her.

"Do you promise not to laugh?" She turned her head up to look at me.

"I would never laugh at anything you wanted, Lia. Ever."

"Okay," she said, sighing heavily. "I forget you're *not* my brother. He has always given me shit about how this isn't a *real* dog."

She took a deep breath and then slowly let it out.

"I want a pomsky."

I pulled my brows together, trying to figure out what kind of dog she was talking about.

"It's a mix between a Pomeranian and a Siberian Husky. They're little and have the cutest little faces! They're black and white and look like they're wearing masks. It's so cute! But they're hard to find and super expensive, so I would probably get something like a lab instead. They're high on my list too, probably because they're always happy and playful."

"I think it sounds cute," I said, hugging her tighter. "What would you name it?"

She tapped her finger to her chin as if she was thinking about it but I knew she already had a name picked out. I could tell that this was something Lia had put a ton of thought into over the years.

"Princess."

"Would you dress her up and make her one of those fancy dogs people carry around in their purses?"

"Probably."

She laughed and laid her head against my chest, making herself comfortable where she was meant to be all along.

<u>Forty</u>
Lia
Two Months Later

"Why can't you tell me what's going on?" I asked as Kensy and Bella guided me out of the car and wrapped a blindfold around my eyes.

"Because it's a surprise," Bella said, pulling it tight before tying it behind my head.

"What kind of surprise?"

"It wouldn't be a surprise if we told you," Kensy scolded playfully. "Now stop asking questions and trying to ruin it."

"Can't you just give me a little hint? This feels a little intense. Could I at least go inside and change out of my scrubs?"

"No. You're fine with what you're wearing. Stop being a baby," Kensy said with a playful tone.

"Watch your step." Bella's arm wrapped around my waist as she guided me up the driveway.

"I really don't like surprises," I complained, my heart racing, not knowing what was waiting for me on the other side.

It wasn't my birthday, so I wasn't expecting a big party waiting for me inside or anything. Still, I couldn't figure out what could possibly be going on that I needed to be intercepted and blindfolded before going inside.

"You'll like this one," Kensy assured me.

"Does it involve Mason waiting for me naked on the couch?"

"I sure hope not," my brother said, taking over and leading me inside.

"Oh, you're here too. Fun." I tried not to be too bitter or sarcastic, but I hated not knowing what was happening.

"I missed you too, sis. So nice to spend time together."

"Whatever, you know how much I hate surprises."

"Yes, but as your friends have already told you, you'll love this one."

"Everyone seems to think they know everything and what I will and won't like, yet no one is willing to let me in on what is happening."

"Just stop worrying about it and allow yourself to enjoy this," my brother whispered, pulling me to a stop, though I had no idea where I was.

Heavenly aromas filled the air, immediately assaulting my senses and making my stomach growl. I didn't have to see anything to recognize the work of Mason and his mouthwatering eggplant parm that I loved so much.

"Hey, baby," he said, stepping in front of me and holding my hands.

"Hi."

"Don't be nervous," he replied, rubbing his hands up and down my arms, which were now tense against my sides.

"Easy for you to say. You're not standing in front of your friends and family wearing a blindfold and having no idea what's going on."

"Let's fix that then. I'll take the blindfold off, but you have to promise me that you'll keep your eyes closed for a few seconds until I tell you to open them. Deal?"

"Fine. Deal." I sighed heavily as if this was the biggest favor to be asked of me, though I was secretly starting to feel the excitement of whatever he was hiding from me.

His fingers brushed against my hair as he undid the blindfold and gently pulled it away from my face.

"Hold out your hands," he instructed. "Keep your eyes closed."

"Okay," I said nervously, putting my hands out in front of me.

My heart beat wildly in my chest as I waited to see what he handed me, but nothing could have prepared me for the warm ball of fluff that was placed in my arms. I gasped, trying not to get my hopes up as I desperately waited for him to let me see.

"Open your eyes, baby."

I did as he asked and immediately began blinking away the tears as I stared down at the most beautiful puppy.

"Oh my gosh!" I squealed, lifting it up and placing it to my face, planting soft kisses along its precious little face.

"Lia, meet Princess," Mason said softly. "Unless you've changed your mind and want to name her something else."

"No," I sobbed, shaking my head and cuddling the sweet girl closer to me. "Princess is perfect."

"Just like you." He pulled me into a hug and squeezed, making sure not to hurt Princess.

"You got me a puppy?" I asked, staring up at him in disbelief.

He nodded, a shy smile playing across his lips.

"Why?"

It wasn't that I didn't want her or that I wasn't thankful for the incredibly sweet gift, but it wasn't anywhere on my radar that he would consider getting a pet.

"Because I have something that I've been wanting to ask you and it just made sense to do both at the same time."

My blood pressure skyrocketed as I pictured Mason dropping to one knee and proposing to me in front of my family and friends. We had agreed to take things slow after our little miscommunication mishap a few months ago, but I hadn't expected that he would suddenly speed things up and ask me to marry him without any sort of warning.

"Stop overthinking this," he warned playfully. "I'm not proposing."

I puffed out the breath I had been holding and pulled Princess tighter against me.

"Sorry," I whispered, looking nervously around at the audience we had watching us in the living room.

"Don't be. We're still taking things slowly and will continue to move at whatever pace works for you, Lia. But that doesn't mean I won't ask for some small things along the way."

"Okay," I stammered nervously, totally confused now.

"Today marks three months since you broke your ankle, and I came rushing over to save you," he said with a smirk.

"I didn't need saving," I corrected.

"You did, especially since *Alexander* didn't bother to respond to your cries for help."

I rolled my eyes, remembering how I had yelled out every *A*-sounding name I could think of to get the voice commands on my phone to work.

"I would have been fine." I shrugged, smiling when Princess licked my nose.

"Maybe. But without me rushing in to save the day like the true hero I am, our love story would have never started. And now, I'll be the first to admit that our story isn't perfect—but that's okay. I love you regardless of any imperfections—"

"Hey now," I warned, laughing as my eyebrows raised. "You're far from perfect, Dr. Dickhead."

"I never claimed to be," he said with a laugh. "But my point is that I love you regardless of how stubborn and violent you might be at times. And while I would have never expected to fall in love the way we did, I wouldn't change it for anything in the world. Our love story is uniquely us, and even though we tend to do things backward, I'd like to make something official."

My eyes widened, wondering if he was going to propose after all. It sure as hell sounded like it, but he just kept smirking at me as if he enjoyed torturing me right now.

"You said that you wanted a puppy since you were a little girl and that having one would make you feel more like an adult," Mason continued, earning a little smile from me as Princess wiggled in my arms, then laid down and went to sleep. "I think you're more than ready for the responsibility of taking care of a pet—far more than caring for a plant, by the way."

I scrunched my nose at him, knowing he was referring to the collection of plants I killed over the summer when I tried to convince him that I could keep a garden alive. Those plants never stood a chance.

"Lia, would you move in with me?" he asked, leaning in to hold up a key that was attached to Princess's collar that I hadn't noticed until now.

I opened my mouth to say something but then snapped it shut, my mind going a mile a minute.

"Just say yes, you already live together," my brother said under his breath from across the room.

"Stop it!" Kensy hissed, making me laugh.

"Yes, Mason. I'll move in with you!"

He grabbed me and pulled me into his chest, placing his lips over mine as everyone clapped for us. Princess shifted in my arms and then fell back asleep, clearly unimpressed with the life-changing moment that just happened.

"You do know that we've been technically living together already, right?" I asked, looking into his beautiful eyes.

"Technically, yes. But I wanted to make it official—which means I want to get all of your stuff moved over here and out of your parent's garage ASAP." He reached down and removed the key from the collar, and then handed it to me.

"You also know that I already had a key, right?" My cheeks hurt from grinning so hard.

"Yeah, but I changed the locks today."

"So what would have happened if I said no?"

"You wouldn't be able to get in the house." He shrugged.

"Mason!" I laughed and shook my head. "You were really going to kick me out onto the streets with Princess if I didn't agree to officially move in?"

"No way. Princess would have stayed here with me."

"You were going to keep my brand new puppy?" I clutched her against my chest and batted my eyes at him.

"Hey, she was a move-in gift. You don't move in, you don't get the gift." He dug his fingers into my hip and pulled me closer.

It was nice not being on crutches anymore and not having to worry about them getting in the way between us.

"I'll remember that," I teased, giving him my best scolding look.

Forty-One
Mason

"Princess needs to go out," I said, nodding to where she was bouncing by the door as I stirred the taco meat in the pan.

"She is obsessed with going outside," Lia complained, bending down to scoop the dog up. "She doesn't even need the restroom, she just wants to run around and get into stuff so I'm forced to give her a bath later."

"Sounds like some princess behavior." I arched an eyebrow, expecting her to call me out on insinuating she was the same, but she didn't. Instead, she took the dog outside and closed the door behind her.

I finished dinner and had everything plated by the time Lia came back inside with Princess. This was our new routine, and I loved that everything felt like it had shifted into place for us. Life was predictable and possibly dull for some, but it was perfectly us. We spent as much time as we could doing the things we loved—watching reality cooking shows and fucking each other's brains out.

"Dinner is ready," I said, coming up behind Lia as she washed her hands in the kitchen sink.

"It smells amazing. Thank you for cooking."

She turned around and wrapped her arms around my neck. I could tell that Lia wasn't concerned with eating right now based on the look she was giving me. It was one I would never get tired of. She closed her eyes and pressed her lips to mine, immediately igniting the flame between us.

I reached down and grabbed her ass, lifting her to my hips. She moaned into my mouth as she deepened the kiss, her hands grabbing at my shirt to pull it off. I carried her to the bedroom and laid her on the bed while I stripped off my clothes.

She sat on her knees, taking her time pulling her shirt up and over her head. Her breasts spilled over the tops of the black lace bra that tried to contain them, my fingers itching to free them and take the pebbled nipple into my mouth.

"You're so fucking beautiful," I said, reaching for her as she pulled away and grinned, making me chase her up the bed.

She stopped and pulled her shorts off, leaving her lace thong on to tease me the way she knew I loved. I grabbed her hips and pinned her in place, gently nipping at the flesh on her round ass as she hissed out a breath.

"Lie down," she demanded, waiting for me to do so before climbing on top.

I reached down and ran a finger along her slit, loving how wet she was already for me. She locked eyes with me as she slid herself along my cock, pressing her panties to the side as she lined me up at her entrance.

The moment Lia was free of her cast, she'd been obsessed with riding my cock every chance she got. We'd fucked in every position we could, working to satisfy the need inside her to be as flexible as she could. But being in control was what turned Lia on the most, and I wasn't about to complain about the insanely hot view I got from watching her tits bounce as she rode herself to climax.

She closed her eyes and tipped her head back, her long neck begging to be kissed. I reached into the nightstand drawer beside me and pulled out the infamous hot pink bullet that had once hit me in the head. Her eyes flicked open as she heard the buzzing noise when I turned it on. She shook her head and grinned, remembering that day as clearly as I did.

I pressed it to her clit and teased her as she increased her speed, rubbing herself against my shaft as she took me deeply inside her. I lifted my hips and matched each thrust, knowing how much it drove her crazy to be fucked like this. Her body tensed above me seconds before she began trembling and falling apart from another intense orgasm.

****

Thank you so much for reading the Beaumont Creek series! I hope you've enjoyed this small-town series as much as I loved creating it! If you're looking for more steamy small-town romance, be sure to check out my Whiskey Mountain series!

Something To Talk About https://books2read.com/u/4X62ag

If you're looking for something more thrilling, be sure to check out the Haven Brook series! It's steamy, small-town romantic suspense that is sure to keep you on the edge of your seat!

'Til Death Do Us Part (Haven Brook Book 1)

https://books2read.com/u/m2RJNR

Other Books By Samantha Baca

The Haven Brook Series
(small-town romantic suspense):

'Til Death Do Us Part (Haven Brook Book 1)

https://books2read.com/u/m2RJNR

The Cradle Will Fall (Haven Brook Book 2)

https://books2read.com/u/b6O0QE

The Ties That Bind (Haven Brook Book 3)

https://books2read.com/u/mqgoz8

A Very Haven Christmas (Haven Brook Book 4- Novella)

https://books2read.com/u/mvqGjj

Three Strikes, You're Gone (Haven Brook Book 5)

https://books2read.com/u/mvqL2z

<u>The Dark Shadows Trilogy</u>
<u>(romantic suspense)</u>

Five Steps Ahead (Dark Shadows Book 1)

https://books2read.com/u/38Q0gO

Ten Seconds Too Late (Dark Shadows Book 2)

https://books2read.com/u/3JRgVB

Against The Clock (Dark Shadows Book 3)

https://books2read.com/u/m2YwoR

<u>The Stone Creek Series</u>
<u>(small-town- novellas)</u>

Chocolate Covered Mistletoe (Stone Creek Book 1)

https://books2read.com/u/3LRk9N

Candy Coated Promises (Stone Creek Book 2)

https://books2read.com/u/mldP5Y

Pumpkin Spiced Possibilities (Stone Creek Book 3)

https://books2read.com/u/bojdwV

<u>Beaumont Creek Series</u>
<u>(small town)</u>

Just One Time (Beaumont Creek Book 1)

https://books2read.com/u/3G52zK

Second Chances (Beaumont Creek Book 2)

https://books2read.com/u/4Aj6Z0

Third Time's The Charm (Beaumont Creek Book 3)

https://books2read.com/u/b5lEyG

Four-ever Single (Beaumont Creek Book 4)

https://books2read.com/u/4j5jMX

Fifth Wheel (Beaumont Creek Book 5)

https://books2read.com/u/4XwKwa

<u>Whiskey Mountain Series</u>
<u>(small-town- novellas)</u>

Something To Talk About

https://books2read.com/u/4X62ag

Something To Think About

https://books2read.com/u/3GWAan

Something To Believe In

https://books2read.com/u/3yVzgB

Something To Live For

https://books2read.com/u/mllEOP

<u>Sugarplum Falls Series</u>
<u>(Holiday Novellas- can be read as standalone)</u>

Blame It On The Mistletoe

https://books2read.com/u/bw1rqe

Blame It On The Eggnog

https://books2read.com/u/38PPY6

Fifth Wheel

Blame It On The Candy Canes

https://books2read.com/u/31DNo7

Blame It On The Blizzard

https://books2read.com/u/b6z6XE

<u>Standalone Books</u>

One Last Wish

https://books2read.com/u/mqg7D9

Finding Love In Apartment 2C (novella)

https://books2read.com/u/bze9aZ

Cocky Counsel: A Hero Club Novel

https://books2read.com/u/31Kzkn

All Is Fair In Food And War (novella)

https://books2read.com/u/bp8qjX

<u>Holiday Books (novellas)</u>

Snow Place To Go

https://books2read.com/u/4A560N

A Christmas Wish

https://books2read.com/u/4EKXpE

Holiday Hijinks

https://books2read.com/u/4DP6Ze

<u>Acknowledgments</u>

Writing a book is hard, but having readers like you makes this journey so rewarding! I can't believe that I have officially published 31 books since I first started in April 2020. There have been so many incredible things that have happened along the way, but none of this would have been possible without the constant love and support I've had along the way. For that, I will always be eternally grateful.

Amanda and Valerie—I cannot begin to fully express the thanks and gratitude that I feel for both of you. You've been by my side, encouraging me when I wanted to give up and offering me the support I needed to keep going. Thank you for constantly spoiling me with your time and pushing me to do better. I love the friendships we've built along the way and could not have written this book without you two.

Claire, Malissa, and Jackie— thank you, ladies, for stepping up when I was in the middle of a crisis and volunteering to read through the book quickly so I didn't miss my deadlines. Your kindness and generosity in helping me does not go unnoticed, and I truly appreciate how easily you all jump in to help when needed. Your feedback is incredibly valuable, and I love that you know my voice so well by now that you keep me on my toes and make sure that each book I put out is the best it can be. Thank you so much for all of your help!

I've said it at least 30 other times—see what I did there? But I honestly couldn't do any of this without the love and support of my family. From giving me time to write to shouting about my books to whoever will listen to them—I see you, and I appreciate you helping me succeed. This road is long, and there's no guarantee of where I'll go, but you all stand by me regardless and continue to support me as if I've already made it. Thank you for loving me so unconditionally and for helping me to live my best life and make my dreams come true.

My dear, sweet husband—you do it all. All the time. There's never a break for you, and yet you never complain about any of it. Thank you for everything you do to make sure I have what I want and need in life and for allowing me to try to do the same for you. I love you so much, and I cannot wait to see what the future brings us as we chase after your dreams.

My girls-- you are no longer babies, and it's always so incredible to see how you support me now that you're older and understand more of what mommy does. I hope that I will always be an inspiration for you to go after your dreams and do the things that you love. That you live fearlessly and passionately. I love you both so much.

To all of the readers who continue to devour my books and preorder them without knowing what they're about—thank you so very much. You've given me life that I didn't know I had inside of me and have allowed me to step outside of my comfort zone to create the stories that live inside of me. Thank you so much for giving my books a chance! I hope they've brought you plenty of joy and an escape from the real world, even if only for a short time.

About the Author

Samantha lives in the southwest with her husband and two small children after abandoning her childhood dream of living in a cabin in Colorado when she found that she couldn't afford to live there and was deathly allergic to the woods. When she's not writing, she's usually spouting off sarcastic remarks while drinking wine out of a coffee mug to look like a functional adult while chasing down her toddlers. She enjoys spending time with her family, watching reruns of Friends, and the 24/7 flow of coffee that can be found in her veins. Be sure to follow her on social media for updates on what she's working on.

You can find her here:

Facebook: https://www.facebook.com/AuthorSamanthaBaca

Instagram: https://instagram.com/author_samantha_baca

Goodreads: http://www.goodreads.com/authorsamanthabaca

Facebook Reader Group:https://www.facebook.com/groups/2945710968775398/

Webpage: https://authorsamanthabaca.wordpress.com

Newsletter: http://eepurl.com/g0NcSj